Dedication

With thanks to the ⟨...⟩
who encouraged m⟨...⟩
especially Mrs. P⟨...⟩
Junior/Middle Schoo⟨...⟩   f
Rosebery School, Epsom; both no longer with us.
The former introduced me to a world I continue
to love; the latter urged me keep my head up, my
imagination sharp, and my writing flowing.

Thank you both.

For all those who still champion creative writing
in schools, and who seek out children with
literary aspirations within a curriculum which
isn't always as flexible as we might wish: please
don't give up. You may never know to whom you
bring life, hope, a refuge, and the satisfaction of
exploring that never-ending world of imagination
through the wonderful gift of creative words.

Other books by Jenny Sanders
Published by The Conrad Press:

The Magnificent Moustache and other stories

Charlie Peach's Pumpkins

and other stories

Charlie Peach's Pumpkins and other stories

Published by The Conrad Press Ltd. in the United Kingdom 2023

Tel: +44(0)1227 472 874

www.theconradpress.com
info@theconradpress.com

ISBN 978-1-915494-90-0

Typesetting and cover design by Michelle Emerson michelleemerson.co.uk

The Conrad Press logo was designed by Maria Priestley

Printed and bound in Great Britain by Clays Ltd, Elcograf S.p.A.

Charlie Peach's Pumpkins

and other stories

Jenny Sanders

Contents

Charlie Peach's Pumpkins

Charlie Peach's Pumpkins

harlie Peach grew melons.

At least, he did in his dreams. He had been inspired by the ones he'd bought from the local market during one long, hot summer. They had tasted so delicious with a squeeze of lemon juice, and just the right amount of brown sugar. He loved their pleasing roundness and sunny yellow skins, as well as their succulent sweetness. However, the climate of southern England does not yet lend itself to the growing of melons, and Charlie was sorely disappointed that his dream of growing them for himself could not become a reality.

Little-Vernon-in-the-Marsh, where he lived, was full of people who grew their own fruit and vegetables. The vicar grew parsnips and beetroot; the school caretaker grew raspberries, strawberries and blueberries; the Women's Institute oversaw a plot which grew lettuces, cabbages, broccoli and sprouts; there was an apple orchard behind the pub, and the school had an entire garden especially funded by the Parents Association, where runner beans flourished alongside peas, potatoes, tomatoes and courgettes. In fact, you didn't have to go very far through Little-Vernon-in-the-Marsh to have come across an entire smorgasbord of Harvest Festival delights.

Nothing ventured, Charlie reluctantly laid his melon plans aside, wrestled on his wellies, picked up his gardening gloves and set out to grow other things instead. He tried carrots, radishes and onions. These all grow quietly beneath the soil; but when Charlie pulled them up a few weeks later, they were a disaster. Unfortunately, the underground worms and slugs had enjoyed them so much that they had devastated his crop. Instead of plump and colourful vegetables, he had a raggedy collection of half-eaten, shrivelled things which looked like sad old balloons, and which went straight to the compost heap. There would be no home-grown anything for Charlie, it seemed. He was bitterly disappointed that this new endeavour had failed so badly. The only thing that seemed to grow well in his garden were weeds.

Poor Charlie; he was on the verge of giving up on gardening entirely and covering his garden with a wooden deck so he didn't even have to look at the weeds anymore.

He was dejectedly contemplating this prospect of this personal defeat one morning, as he sat nervously in Mr. McCavity's waiting room, where he was due his six monthly dental check-up. Now, a lot of dentists keep a variety of (usually very old) magazines for their clients to read; this one was no exception. They are a good distraction when you are about to have someone poke about in your mouth with their face so close to yours that you can feel their hot breath on your cheeks. Mr. McCavity knew this too, so he not only provided a selection of reading material, but sensibly ensured that he always had a supply of breath mints in his own medical coat pocket.

Picking up a magazine at random, Charlie came across an article which soon had him totally engrossed. It was written by a farmer in Morton, Illinois, a place in America; a place which, Charlie learned, was known as *The Pumpkin Capital Of The World*.

Charlie was very impressed. Imagine if his garden had come to be known as *The Melon Capital Of Little-Vernon-in-the-Marsh*. That would have been amazing! He was slowly coming to terms with the fact that that dream was permanently shattered;

but the more he read, the more Charlie liked the idea of pumpkins. After all, they were not so very different from melons; to look at, at least. They had that same big, beautiful shape and the wonderful colours of a summer sunset. Perhaps, he pondered, his garden could become *The Pumpkin Capital Of Little-Vernon-in-the-Marsh*. It had a nice ring to it.

The more he read, the more excited he became.

Charlie found out about mulching, nurturing, and harvesting pumpkins. He read about planting them in mounds of soil so that the drainage was good; about polythene tunnels to keep the destructive insects off them until after the plants had flowered. He learned about pollination, correct watering methods – don't let them get too soggy – and how to prune them if you wanted to grow a couple of giant pumpkins rather than a wheelbarrow full of average sized ones. There were paragraphs about growing the plants on straw to keep the moisture in the soil; and about slipping cardboard under the expanding spheres so that they didn't go rotten before they were ready to pick. The detailed article was enhanced by glossy photographs of enormous pumpkins you could roast, or steam, or make into soups, or even into pies (the Americans seemed especially fond of these). You could use them to decorate your house, or a dining table for a special autumnal feast; or, you could scoop them out, and carve elaborate shapes into them to turn them into lanterns for Halloween.

Charlie was exhilarated by the thought of finally growing something so impressive, and he began to imagine his own dining room table decorated with orange orbs, and his front porch strewn with the fruits of his labour. He became determined that in the one hundred days that the article told him it took to grow a pumpkin from a seed to a big, football-sized vegetable, he would make his dream a reality.

His enthusiasm for the idea grew to such a pitch, that Charlie absent-mindedly rolled up the magazine, thrust it into his pocket – knocking several other publications to the floor as he got up – and left the dental surgery in a flurry of anticipation. All thoughts of Mr. McCavity's prods, pokes, drills, fillings and check-ups vanished from his thoughts as, without a backward glance and without waiting to be called for his appointment, he headed straight back home.

The dentist watched him scurry past the window, just as he was carefully filling his current patient's mouth with wodges of those little tubes of cotton wool that absorb moisture.

'I wonder where he's off to in such a hurry?' Mr. McCavity mused, out loud.

'Pffffmmhgmmff,' burbled the poor patient, whose mouth was now as dry as the Sahara desert, and whose strangled sounds could have meant almost anything.

Once home, Charlie unfolded the now somewhat crumpled magazine and studied the form you could fill in to order seeds. He was dazzled by the sheer quantity and variety which were available to buy. He'd had no idea there were so many different types of pumpkin to choose from: big and small, smooth or bumpy; there were green and white pumpkins as well as the usual orange kind. He chose a variety called *Autumn Golden* which, the description reliably informed him, would be great for carving as well as eating and would, just as the article had said, take one hundred days to grow. He filled in the form online to save time, and hit 'send' with a satisfied sigh of achievement. Now all he had to do was wait for them to arrive.

In fact, the next few days saw a flurry of activity in Charlie Peach's garden as he prepared the ground ready to sow his pumpkin seeds into the rich, dark soil. His neighbour, who also happened to be the local vicar, Reverend Patmos, enjoyed peeking over the fence from time to time to observe the progress.

'All right there, Charlie?' he would enquire as he took a well-deserved break from studying for the next Sunday sermon, and checked on his parsnips and beetroot while enjoying a breath of fresh air with his morning coffee.

'Grand thanks,' Charlie would reply, and each would return to their tasks, glad to have exchanged a friendly greeting.

This scene was repeated daily for the next ten days, until the pumpkin seeds arrived; then Charlie buried each one carefully into the mounds of earth he had prepared. He placed the polythene cloches over them with the same tenderness as you might tuck a baby into their cot at night. In fact, had you been listening closely, you might have heard Charlie Peach singing softly to his plants as he checked on them each morning and evening.

I don't know whether you have ever visited Little-Vernon-in-the-Marsh; if you have, you will know that it's a quiet sort of place, where people are busy with life but don't generally make a fuss. Not a great deal goes on there apart from the school summer play, which is always sold out, and the annual Christmas market. So, it will come as no surprise to you to hear that everyone in the village was agog to discover whether Charlie's pumpkin venture would be a success.

Yes, word had got out that he was doing something rather out of the ordinary. Instead of calling on him themselves, the villagers found excuses to visit the Vicar next door. They contrived clever ruses to have him take them into his garden, and then peered over the fence on Charlie's side to see for themselves what all the hubbub was about.

As word spread, it was not long before the local paper, *The Vernon Voice*, based in Vernon-on-the-Moor, got involved. This weekly publication was delivered across the area to a number of villages including Little-Vernon-in-the-Marsh, Greater

Vernon, Vernon-by-Clevedon, Upper Vernon, Lower Vernon and of course, Vernon-on-the-Moor. They operated with a small team of three journalists, one of whom was usually an intern studying a journalism course, who could gain valuable experience for a few months. The stories the paper published were usually about football matches; cats stuck in trees; why no-one had emptied the bins in the park recently; surveys about car parking charges, and a few columns for advertising things people wanted to buy or sell. The editor was always on the look out for something rather more interesting, and preferably dramatic – a juicy murder or a gang of international jewel thieves, perhaps – but she struggled to find any events of that nature anywhere in the vicinity of the Vernons.

Naturally however, when word reached the paper about Charlie's pumpkins, enquiries were made and someone was sent to write it all up for the next edition.

Michelle Boot, was the intern who arrived on Charlie's doorstep about nine weeks after he had planted his pumpkin patch. She was on a six month international placement from America, and was loving every minute of it. Her home town, in the States, was a sprawling mass of concrete office blocks, factories and industrial buildings; the English countryside was captivating for her. She loved the way the green fields spread like a patchwork quilt across the countryside, and the way the winding hedges provided natural corridors for scurrying creatures and nesting birds.

Charlie Peach didn't know very much about America, apart from the inspiring article he'd so recently read at Mr. McCavity's dental surgery. He'd never travelled there and had never met an American before either; he'd just seen them on television and in films.

He didn't like the way they called trousers 'pants', or pavements 'sidewalks', or a car boot a 'trunk'; or an honest-to-goodness biscuit a 'cookie', for that matter. It was very confusing.

He found their accent hard to understand and, added to that, Charlie was cautious about most things new and different; except for his pumpkins which were already bringing him a great deal of pleasure.

He was therefore, somewhat alarmed when he opened his front door to be greeted by a red-headed girl in a blue baseball cap with a large camera hanging around her neck, and an interesting accent.

'Charlie Peach?' she enquired with her head on one side; squinting from the bright, early September sunshine.

'That would be me,' Charlie affirmed. 'Can I help you?'

'I'm sure you can, sir. I'm Michelle Boot. I'm with *The Vernon Voice* noospaper.'

There was no answer. Mr. Peach looked baffled. Michelle fiddled with the badge on her jacket

which said *I heart England*. She peered out from beneath her cap and continued, 'The noospaper phoned you, sir. Sir…?'

Charlie was astonished; he simply stood on the front step with his mouth open. He was not a fan of baseball caps – he liked a good old-fashioned trilby himself, preferably in tweed – but, to his surprise, he did quite like being called, 'sir'.

Michelle Boot frowned a little. As you are well aware, none of us enjoys being stared at by someone we've never met before, and especially one who insists on standing in front of us with their mouth open. Michelle was no exception and she began to wonder whether he was quite well.

'Of course;' Charlie recovered his manners just before things got truly awkward, and feeling somewhat embarrassed, he invited her in and indicated a chair.

'I'm here to look at your pumpkins, sir,' Michelle said, pulling a notebook out of her backpack and a pen from behind her ear. 'I hear you have quite a story to tell regarding growing things in your back yard.'

Poor Charlie didn't understand her.

'I don't have a yard, I'm afraid. Just a little patch of garden really.'

'Sure,' his guest nodded, 'a garden. Garden. That's it. Can I see it? Maybe take some photographs? My Grandpa used to grow pumpkins back home in the States. I love 'em!'

Charlie led his young guest through the house and out of the back door to the garden, where his pumpkin plants were flourishing. In fact, they were the only thing that was flourishing at all, because Charlie had pulled up every other bush, shrub and flower that had been busy growing there between those infernal weeds, to make space for his wonderful pumpkins.

He had given some straggly rhubarb plants to Reverend Patmos next door, who loved an apple and rhubarb tart smothered in custard during the cold winter months; and a couple of struggling shrubs to the school, where an over enthusiastic beagle had dug up the ones that used to grow outside the Headmistress' office and chewed them to bits. She had been profoundly grateful.

The pumpkins were already on day sixty-two; the plastic cloches were gone now, and it wouldn't be long before the little round growths would start to look like less like marbles and more like real pumpkins.

The would-be journalist uncapped her camera and began taking photographs of the garden; some with Charlie and some without. It soon became clear that Michelle Boot knew quite a bit about pumpkins herself, and before long Charlie forgot about baseball caps and even began to understand her accent better. He was soon telling her all about his dream to grown melons and how it hadn't worked out. He talked about the carrot, radish and onion experiment; and how disastrous that endeavour had been. She asked good questions, and switched between writing notes on her pad and recording him on her phone as he explained how he had come across the article in Mr. McCavity's waiting room, and the fresh energy he had now that he had switched from melons to pumpkins.

She nodded and wrote; wrote and nodded; saying things like 'Uh ha'; 'All righty'; 'No way!'; and, 'Is that right?'

She was a good listener, and Charlie found he was even telling her that his new, ambitious dream was that his pumpkin patch might one day become, *The Pumpkin Capital Of Little-Vernon-in-the-Marsh*.

Michelle didn't laugh; she didn't even giggle; she thought it was a great dream. She understood that the growing of pumpkins is a serious business. She liked Charlie; she was drawn to his honesty; she admired him for not giving up on his dream. In her culture people always seemed to dream about almost impossible things, like being astronauts, famous movie stars or rock musicians, which often required them to compete with other ambitious people in a way that always left someone feeling sad, hurt, and not-quite-good-enough. Charlie wasn't full of himself like that; he was just full of pumpkin dreams and big ideas, and he was putting his ideas into action. She found it very appealing and besides, he reminded her of her grandpa who had passed away a few years ago, and who she missed enormously. She found being in Charlie's pumpkin-filled garden curiously comforting.

'Perhaps I could come back and follow the story as they grow? Maybe again, after that when Fall begins?' she asked.

'Fall?' Charlie repeated, puzzled. 'I don't think they *fall* off: I'll have to pick them; or cut them from their vines when they're ready.'

Michelle smiled.

'Sure; sorry. I mean autumn. When the leaves are falling off the trees. Your pumpkins should be good and ready about then.'

'Ah,' breathed Charlie, highly relieved and realising this was another Americanism. The thought of a whopping great pumpkin falling on top of him had made him feel rather anxious. 'I'd like that,' he said warmly, delighted at her interest.

He hadn't found anyone who shared his new fascination with pumpkins until now. Of course, lots of people had enjoyed peering over the fence from Reverend Patmos's garden; but they had just been nosy, which isn't the same thing at all. People had asked him questions about what he was doing too, but he could tell they were just making conversation so they could pass on information to other village gossips. The Vicar himself had seemed more interested in the rhubarb Charlie had given him than in the pumpkins. Michelle however, was genuinely fascinated by the project, and it was good to find someone who shared his interest.

'Would you like a cup of tea before you go?' he offered, heading back inside to fill the kettle.

'That'd be great, thanks.' Michelle bit her lip thoughtfully. 'Could you just give me a moment though.'

Charlie could see she had something on her mind.

'I'd just like to take a couple more pictures while I'm here, to be sure I have enough. Are you OK with that?'

Charlie nodded before busying himself with mugs, milk, sugar and tea bags, placing them on a tray – something he very rarely bothered with when he was on his own.

Michelle seemed to be taking her time. What on earth was she doing out there? Surely she was just taking pictures of his pumpkins; really, that shouldn't take this long, should it?

The kettle had boiled and the tea was brewing nicely when Michelle finally came back from the garden repinning her badge to her jacket.

'All done!' she announced.

Charlie had his head in the cupboard, rummaging for a packet of biscuits amongst the jars, and bottles. He emerged to see her politely wiping her feet on the back door mat.

'Thanks, Charlie; this has been swell. You know what though; I should run. I gotta make some calls about a dog show over in Upper Vernon, and I need to swing by the garage for gas first.'

She shook Charlie's hand and, after a quick swig of hot tea, left in a whirl of notes and ideas, leaving Charlie with a plate full of oat and raisin biscuits, and wondering why she could possibly want gas.

Charlie's days were now full of pumpkiny things. His garden was looking more and more orange as the pumpkins grew and grew. They needed

to be watered regularly – not too much, but not too little. He hauled a load of manure back home from the local stables in his wheelbarrow, to help the pumpkins grow even bigger and faster. Sure enough, their girths were expanding rapidly, but Charlie was sure they could do better. After all, if his garden was ever to become *The Pumpkin Capital of Little-Vernon-in-the-Marsh*, they needed to be truly spectacular.

Charlie read everything that he could lay his hands on about pumpkins. He cycled to the library in Vernon-on-the-Moor to search their extensive gardening section. He listened to *Gardeners' Question Time*, to glean new tips; he even typed his own questions into his computer and learned that plants enjoy music.

Scientists have discovered that the sound waves and vibrations of some music can stimulate growth in plant cells. This was exciting news, and Charlie lost no time in experimenting for himself. He tried different kinds of music: rap, rock, ballads, hip-hop, reggae, disco, jazz, classical. He played music from his radio, balancing it on his wheelie bin and covering it with a well-positioned umbrella when it rained.

He kept thorough notes and drew graphs to record pumpkin growth, noting their weekly progress, but was disappointed to find that playing music hadn't made much difference. Until, that is, he accidentally tuned into a radio station playing country music. His pumpkins loved it!

Suddenly Charlie found himself marking multiple growth spurts on his graph. He wondered what the scientists would say about that. Perhaps the seeds themselves still had something of the American south inside them, and were simply responding to the music of their original homeland. It was a curious thought. Those scientist should certainly look into it more thoroughly.

Reverend Patmos enjoyed it too.

'You know, Charlie,' the Vicar commented one morning while nodding his head in time to the song on the radio, 'you should really have some sort of pumpkin celebration. They're coming along so nicely. Americans celebrate Thanksgiving every November and have pumpkins all over the place for that.' He paused reflectively. 'Gratitude is increasingly rare, I find. I wonder why that is...'

'Sure, Charlie,' Michelle encouraged him when Charlie told her about this conversation.

It was day eighty-one, and she'd called in to update her report, take a few more photographs and see how things were going.

'This is a patch to be proud of.' She gave a low whistle. 'My Grandpa would be impressed if he could see it. Your first year, and these are real beauts.'

Charlie blushed and glowed with pride all at once. The pumpkins certainly did look magnificent. In fact, they had succeeded all his expectations.

'These will soon be ready for harvest,' she continued. 'Whatcha gonna do with them all?'

This was a very good question. Charlie had been awake for the past several nights pondering this very thing. He had hundreds of mature pumpkins which he now had absolutely no idea what to do with. It had just been a hopeful dream all those weeks ago when he was sitting in the dentist's waiting room; but now that it had become a reality, what on earth *was* he going to do with so many pumpkins? He'd had so many failures in his garden, deep down he had honestly expected this would prove to be another.

Genuinely perplexed, he turned to Michelle with a look of abject panic on his face.

A quick calculation had told him that even if every family in the village had one, he'd still have a mountain of them left over. If he made them all into soup, he'd need to buy several huge freezers to store it all, as well as a giant cauldron to cook it. That was impractical and expensive. He wondered vaguely whether any local restaurants would like to offer a winter special of pumpkin soup… all year round…

Michelle laughed.

'Ya know, I could help you out Charlie. How about that celebration the Pastor suggested? It could be a cross between harvest and Thanksgiving. A nice event for all the Vernons, perhaps.'

Charlie nodded, eagerly grabbing at this germ of an idea.

'I know you don't do Thanksgiving in England, Charlie; but you could have an autumn festival right here in your back yard or even better, on the village green. Maybe make some pumpkin pie and such. I'm sure the noospaper could advertise it for you, and there's a bunch of people who'd be glad to help.'

Charlie's brain was foggy, but Michelle's idea was like a light at the end of a dark tunnel.

'Hey Charlie!' Michelle clicked her fingers in front of him. 'Are you with me? Come on, Charlie; we could do it together,' she suggested. 'I'm sure the folks around here would love a big autumn event. We could get everyone involved; maybe the paper could sponsor a band. Someone round here must play country music. It'll be something to look forward to before Christmas. Besides, I have to go back to America before December 25th, so I'll miss your celebrations and local traditions.'

Despite feeling overwhelmed and a little light-headed, it was dawning on Charlie that although her ideas were rather ambitious, this was an excellent solution, and Michelle just might have the drive to help pull it off.

'All right,' he agreed nervously; grateful for both the idea and the encouragement.

'Just gotta go check on my favourite pumpkin before I leave,' Michelle said.

Charlie wasn't aware that Michelle had a favourite pumpkin. She quickly disappeared into the garden again, leaving Charlie to make a list of things they might need in order to hold an autumn festival in Little-Vernon-on-the-Marsh, including permission from the Parish Council – the Vicar would know about that.

She was back in a few minutes looking very pleased with herself. Charlie raised his eyebrows in a questioning look. What was it she was really busy with out there?

'All on track, Charlie. I'm heading back to the office to rustle up some advertising. You pick a date and let's get this show on the road.'

Charlie smiled. He didn't really understand some of the things Michelle said, but he did enjoy her enthusiasm.

By the next week, permission had been granted, a date chosen, and notices were appearing on the lampposts throughout the Vernon regions, announcing the Pumpkin Festival to be held on the village green before the month was out. There was a full page advertisement in *The Vernon Voice*, including information on pumpkin carving printed underneath a huge headline declaring:

Are You Pumped For Pumpkins?

This was followed by a news feature, written by Michelle, including details and tips on choosing a pumpkin of your own from Charlie's garden patch. There were posters positioned on roundabouts and displayed in front gardens, full of information about the festival.

Everyone agreed that it was lovely to have something fun to look forward to now the days were gradually getting shorter and darker. Halloween was a bit too spooky for some people in the community. Old people were, understandably, frightened by masked ghouls and ghosts at their doors. Mr. McCavity quite enjoyed it; he always had a full appointment book afterwards when a rush of patients booked in, all needing fillings after the excess sugar they'd scoffed on their *Trick or Treat* circuit. (He was, however, very careful not to let his own children take part in that activity; they were given fresh fruit and colouring books.) Firework Night was a bit too loud and scary for anyone with pets, so Charlie's Pumpkin Festival was much more to their liking.

One bright morning, the postman delivered a book to Charlie's house entitled *100 & 1 things you never knew you could do with a pumpkin*. It was a real eye-opener, and came with a note from Michelle saying: 'Let's go, Charlie!'

Not many days later, Charlie could be seen carrying an armful of huge pumpkins from the garden and moving around his kitchen with all the intent of someone on a serious mission. Indeed, he was cooking up a storm with recipes from Michelle's book, but had always known that he had too many pumpkins, as well as too many recipes, to make all by himself.

It was Michelle who suggested contacting the Women's Institute and the school. A host of capable and interesting ladies from the WI swooped to the rescue, dividing the recipes between themselves. Michelle insisted on choosing the pumpkins for them, which Charlie thought was a bit strange; he couldn't understand why she was so mysterious about it, but he was too busy to wonder about it for long.

The entire school had been busy making autumn-themed bunting, which was to be strung up between the trees. The caretaker would supervise an arrangement of tables and chairs, and teachers racked their brains for pumpkiny activities to entertain everyone. The art club made posters; the choir learnt a special song composed by the music department; the science club organised a 'Guess the weight of the pumpkin' stall, and the Parents Association set up a face-painting booth. Mr. Marshall, a gentleman who ran crafting evening classes at the Vernon-on-the Moor library, sharpened his collection of special knives ready to oversee a pumpkin carving competition. Hay bales were positioned in front of an impressive stage, sponsored by *The Vernon Voice*, where a country band would play their music.

Such was the generous spirit of the combined Vernons, that before long the village green was transformed from a quiet, tranquil space into a hub of activity with a strong country theme. Everyone was very excited.

The day of the festival dawned crisp and clear. Charlie's garden was no longer the verdant site of multiple orange growth, since most of the pumpkins were now transformed into culinary delights, while others were piled up in pyramids for people to buy. There were just a couple nestling by the far fence, looking quite lonely in an expanse of earth. Michelle must have missed those ones, Charlie thought to himself, as he washed, shaved, and dressed.

He felt a mixture of excitement, nerves and relief. Charlie had actually had more than one torturous night when he dreamed that evil unicorns had squashed every pumpkin he'd grown and the festival had been ruined before it began. Thank goodness that nightmare hadn't come true. Now he was ready for the big day.

And what a day it was! The green was soon seething with people. The bunting fluttered merrily, the tables and chairs filled with visitors, and the air was filled with squeals of delight. Some people bought pumpkins to take home, and were stuffing them into their cars so they wouldn't have to carry them all day. Others were already carving designs of various levels of intricacy and skill, under the watchful eye of Mr. Marshall. The school caretaker was offering a game of skittles rolling unpredictable pumpkins instead of the usual balls, which was drawing a group of eager teenagers.

A marquee had been erected to house all the wonderful goodies baked, boiled and braised by the resourceful ladies of the Vernon parishes. They were doing a lively trade in fresh pumpkin pancakes and pumpkin waffles, all served with a dollop of pumpkin ice cream. On one side of the green, a coffee catering van was serving spiced pumpkin lattes as fast as they could. Elsewhere, a brightly coloured stall sold jars of pumpkin spread and pumpkin pasta sauce.

Michelle was there, bright and breezy as ever, greeting the locals and serving portions of pumpkin pie as if her life depended on it. Another stall offered all shapes and sizes of pumpkin bread and pumpkin cakes, which were selling fast. And, of course, there were vats of the pumpkin soup which Charlie had made himself. Everyone loved it!

Word had spread far and wide, and people travelled for miles to enjoy the first Autumn Pumpkin Festival. They all recognised Charlie from his picture in the paper, and wherever he turned he was greeted warmly. It seemed that Charlie had become quite famous almost overnight.

Reverend Patmos shook him enthusiastically by the hand.

'Well done, old chap. This is simply marvellous! What a wonderful initiative. You've really pulled off something quite outstanding, my friend. I'm so glad; this is just what we all needed and a great way to pull everyone together.'

Michelle had sold every last slice of pie, and came to find him. She flung her arms round him in a big hug.

'Charlie, you did it!'

He shook his head and turned an interesting shade of red.

'No, Michelle. I think you did it.'

'Sure, Charlie,' she laughed and shook her head back at him. 'OK; I think it's safe to say we did it together, right? You got yourself a great community here ya know.' She looked around the bustling green where families and laughter were mingling in the autumn sunshine. 'I just wish my Grandpa could be here to see this.'

There was a tear in Charlie's eye as he listened to her kind words.

This was one American he would miss very much. Michelle had been so kind to him and so supportive; so different from what he had imagined. He was ashamed now of how he had felt that first day she'd called on him. Now he wished he could have met her grandfather too. Charlie was certain that he would have been a wonderful gentleman. They could have shared pumpkin stories together.

'Don't cry now, Charlie,' she reproached him.

Then, jamming her baseball hat firmly on her head again, she continued, 'I haven't gone yet. Besides, I've got another surprise for you; don't go anywhere.'

Michelle scurried off towards the house, just as the Vicar came by again. Together, they surveyed the scene before them full of smiling, chattering people; adults and children having the most enormous fun and enjoying the fruits of Charlie's labours.

Reverend Patmos turned to his neighbour, 'So Charlie, what do you think you'll grow next year?'

Charlie chuckled. He had no plans to return to shrivelled carrots and hole-ridden onions, that was for sure. Of course, in the spring he could start all over again.

'I think I'll be sticking with pumpkins from now on,' he told the Vicar. 'After all, why be a one year wonder?'

'As I hoped,' the Vicar smiled. 'In that case, the Parish Council and I would like to talk to you about holding this festival every year and expand on your success. It's a big hit with everyone, and such a great way to bring our communities together. It will let people know that Little-Vernon-in-the-Marsh is more than just a small, sleepy village.'

Charlie beamed, partly with pleasure, partly with pride, and partly because he knew that Reverend Patmos was absolutely right.

The Vicar was suddenly distracted, looking over Charlie's shoulder to something happening on the edge of the green. He frowned.

'I think there's someone here to see you.'

Charlie doubted that.

A man with a huge camera was striding across the grass, accompanied by a girl with an equally big, hairy microphone, alongside a second man in a suit matched with an orange patterned tie. From the other direction, a lady with a large clipboard was hurrying towards him calling his name.

'Mr. Peach? Mr. Peach?'

Charlie was sandwiched between them and felt momentarily alarmed. What on earth was going on now?

'Mr. Peach? My name is Harriet James. I'm with *The County Times*. We heard there was something big going on here today, and it seems we were right. I'd love to get a quote.'

The county newspaper? This was a publication with a much wider readership than *The Vernon Voice*. Charlie was amazed. From the other direction, the man in the orange tie – were those pumpkins on it? Charlie thought they were – began talking.

'*Local News at 6*. We got a tip off about today. People have been talking about this event in the studio all week. We'd like to do a feature on the weekend slot. All fine for a quick interview, Charlie?'

At that exact moment Michelle came running up breathlessly, with a pumpkin under her arm.

'Oh Charlie; the band are here. They wanna start. They're waiting for you to make a speech.' In one swift glance she took in the new arrivals. 'Oh yeah; forgot to tell ya, there's some other folks who are real keen to hear about your pumpkin patch. I made a few calls…'

Charlie didn't know what to say. No one had said anything about television, let alone a speech. What would he say in front of all these people with their cameras and microphones; it was like another nightmare he used to have about speaking in public. Suddenly he was overrun with nerves; his tummy felt most peculiar.

'Don't worry, Charlie,' Michelle squeezed his hand encouragingly. 'I'll come with ya.'

So saying, she led him to the stage and tapped the mic.

'Good afternoon Little-Vernon-in-the-Marsh!' There was a feeble cheer. 'Oh; and good afternoon everyone from all the other Vernons.' The crowd appreciated this more, and the volume of their cheer increased. 'Ladies and gentlemen, *The Vernon Voice* is proud to have sponsored this wonderful event. Please welcome with me, the founder of the first ever Little-Vernon-in-the-Marsh Pumpkin Festival;' she paused dramatically. Americans are very good at this sort of thing. 'Charlieeeeee.….. Peeeeeach!' The crowd roared their approval and the team from the television news quickly swung their equipment into action, while *The County Times* lady started taking rapid notes.

Charlie stepped forward nervously and looked out over the throng of people all enjoying the marvellous festival. Who would have thought, way back when he wanted to grow melons and had such a terrible time with those wretched carrots, radishes and onions, that he'd make such a success of pumpkins? He could hardly believe it himself.

He spied Mr. McCavity with his wife and children and momentarily froze as he realised that he had not only left this esteemed gentleman in the lurch some months ago, but stolen a magazine from his waiting room. He was hit with an unwelcome surge of embarrassment at how rude the dentist must have thought him. He immediately resolved to make another appointment as soon as possible.

In spite of his nerves, Charlie managed to thank everyone for coming, all those who'd helped make the festival possible and wished everyone well. Michelle, who was clapping enthusiastically next to him, had a special mention too; after all, it was she who had really inspired the day.

Just as the band were about to launch into their playlist, Michelle, still clutching a pumpkin under one arm, took the mic herself.

'I just want to thank y'all too. Thanks for welcoming me into your community these past few weeks. My internship is done and I have to head back to the States real soon. It's been a treat to get to know some of you and be part of life in this little bit of England.' She looked quite teary and there was a ripple of appreciative applause. She waved her hand; she wasn't finished yet.

'Most of all, I want to thank Charlie who's given me a flavour of home and reminded me that we should never give up. My Grandpa would be real proud today to see what fine pumpkins can be grown beyond Illinois.'

She sniffed loudly and lifted the pumpkin she'd been carrying so it was level with her chest. Slowly, she turned it around. There was a murmur amongst the crowd as everyone saw, etched into the skin the clear words, *DREAM BIG*.

'I scratched these words into this pumpkin with the pin of my badge, when it was no bigger than my fist, the very first time I visited Charlie's garden,' Michelle announced. 'I checked on it every time I came by, and watched the words grow, just as his dream grew into reality. I thought it would be a good reminder for him. And Charlie,' she turned to her new friend, 'I think we can safely say that your big dream has truly turned your back yard into *The Pumpkin Capital Of Little-Vernon-in-the-Marsh*. Congratulations!'

'Three cheers for Charlie!' called out the Vicar; and the crowd responded while the journalists scribbled down the phrase, *The Pumpkin Capital Of Little-Vernon-in-the-Marsh*.

'Thank you,' Charlie mouthed with sincerity as he took the pumpkin from Michelle and held it above his head, like the champion he was.

Later that evening, as he slipped his feet into his slippers and sank gratefully into his armchair with a cup of tea, Charlie gave a deep and satisfied sigh. At the same moment, he heard the soft flap of his

letterbox, put down his drink, and went to see what had been delivered. On the doormat lay the hot-off-the-press edition of *The County Times*.

Unfolding it, he saw a grainy photograph of himself holding up the pumpkin Michelle had given him. There were the words, *DREAM BIG*, in large, clear letters for everyone to read. Below it the headline blazed:

Little Vernon-in-the-Marsh:The Pumpkin Capital of the South West!

Charlie gasped. He could barely believe it. This was simply astounding. The capital – not just of the village, or even the county, but the entire south west of the country. It was beyond everything he had dreamed.

Chuckling to himself, he returned to his armchair reflecting on the extraordinary day with a smile on his face, and contentment in his heart.

'Sometimes,' he said out loud, to no-one in particular, 'your dreams just aren't big enough.'

Wooing Carletia

Wooing Carletia

Kit Armitage looked at himself approvingly in the mirror. He took a deep breath, pulled back his shoulders and liked what he saw. As an ex-RAF man he knew how to stand tall, how to wear his suit with flair, and how to inspire both calm and confidence – just as well since he now worked in the Foreign Office. Today he would need these qualities in abundance, plus a good dose of old-fashioned courage, as he had an appointment with the Prime Minister.

Half an hour later, he was being ushered into a plush office at Number 10 Downing Street, where the thick carpet and curtains sucked all other sounds into themselves, and the leather book-lined walls seemed to murmur knowledge and tradition in equal parts. He was somewhat surprised to find himself alone, but even as he considered that, the Prime Minister himself swept in from a door disguised to look like another bookcase, and plonked several coloured files on a large mahogany desk which dwarfed all the other furniture in the room.

'Kit!' he exclaimed, 'Splendid to see you! Sorry about all this…,' he gestured vaguely at the piles of papers covering the antique blotter and threatening to cascade onto the floor. 'Lots going on, you know. Always is, ha! But you know all about that.'

Kit was just about to agree politely, but the Prime Minister cleared his throat so noisily it would have drowned out any reply, and then rushed on.

'Glad you could pop in. Won't take long. All good news for you.'

The Prime Minister finally took off his glasses and looked up and into the eyes of his guest before beginning to clean the lenses on a silk handkerchief which he had pulled flamboyantly from his top pocket.

'Oh yes; quite perfect. Kit, I am pleased to announce that we are assigning you as our new Ambassador to Carletia. Hmmm, yes indeed.'

The Prime Minister paused again, presumably for dramatic effect, and was gratified to see Kit open both his eyes and his mouth rather wider than was strictly necessary, as his brain began to catch up with this new turn of events.

'Prime Minister, I am honoured,' Kit began.

'Yes indeed. Absolutely. Of course you are. It's a first class posting in every way and I am absolutely delighted for you. Last chap… well, didn't end too well; not to worry. No good crying over spilt milk and all that. Press on! All approved by the Palace of course. In fact, let me be the first to congratulate you.'

Replacing his glasses on his rather sweaty nose, the Prime Minister grabbed the newly appointed

Ambassador's hand and pumped it up and down in hearty best wishes.

By the time Kit left the office, his mind was reeling and his arms were filled with files, photocopies and envelopes, each bursting with the information he would need in order to be thoroughly acquainted with the situation in Carletia. To represent one's country abroad is a fine thing indeed but, truth to tell, after all his years whizzing through the skies with the RAF, he had been enjoying having his feet firmly tucked under the table in his own country cottage of late, and was quite nervous about what would be required in this new role. However, it would be bad form to say, 'No' to the PM, or to the palace for that matter.

Putting aside his personal preferences, Kit Armitage scurried home to pack his things, cancel the milk and newspaper deliveries and, within a week, he found himself in the ambassador's residence in Bregga, capital city of Carletia.

He hadn't had time to make so much as a cup of tea before he was inundated with queries from the staff – secretaries, officials, heads of departments for industry, agriculture, social care, administration, military attachés, naval attachés, housekeepers, drivers and maintenance staff. The embassy was buzzing with excitement at the arrival of Ambassador Armitage.

Kit was mightily relieved that everyone in Carletia spoke English; it certainly made things more straightforward. He had yet to discover what had happened to the last Ambassador; curiously, that information hadn't been in any of the files. Had he been struck down ill, or forced to leave by some family emergency, perhaps? No one had enlightened him on this topic, and Kit was soon fully occupied trying to work his way through a mountain of paperwork and familiarise himself with his new surroundings. On his first morning he had got hopelessly lost in the residence trying to find his way from the bathroom to the office and had to be redirected several times by various secretaries.

There were meetings, meetings and more meetings. Everything took so long, and involved hours of talking to all sorts of important people who, without exception, drank litres of coffee and munched through biscuits as if they were going out of fashion. By the end of the first week he had only one conclusion: things were in a mess. Not just a quick flick-of-a-duster-run-round-with-the-vacuum-cleaner kind of mess. No, no; it became increasingly obvious that things had been neglected here for far too long, and it would take a great deal of time and effort to sort them out. What in the world had been going on?

'Ah,' said the chargé d'affaires, who had been temporarily running the embassy until Kit arrived, when there was finally time to ask on the next Monday morning.

Archibald Grant was a balding man in his late 50s, with an extraordinary quantity of hair growing from his ears which Kit thought most off-putting. He found himself staring in a fashion which was far from polite and had to keep concentrating on the man's nose instead, although the more he focused there, the more it appeared that this was also a source of prolific hair growth. The man would never have got away with this lack of grooming in the RAF, that was for sure.

In an effort to break out of his distracted trance and get his blood circulating again, Kit rotated his tired shoulders with a crack. He was looking for a significantly better answer than, 'Ah.' He looked over the top of his reading glasses at the man, with a look he hoped communicated authority, and raised his eyebrows expectantly. Mr. Grant cleared his throat.

'Well, your Excellency,' for this is how ambassadors are formally addressed. (Kit hadn't got used to that yet; in fact it made him squirm, but he would just have to get used to it.)

'Your Excellency,' the man repeated, 'unfortunately the former occupant of this office was unavoidably required elsewhere.'

'I see,' replied Kit, who didn't see at all. 'And this was...?'

'Some time ago, Sir. In fact, we have been trundling along here like this for almost... er... twenty years.'

'Twenty years?!' The new Ambassador was incredulous. How was that possible?

Mr. Grant continued, 'Even before that, there were... well... signs of a decreased output, one might say.'

'Might one?' enquired Kit, slightly sarcastically. He knew there was more to this story, and that he just wasn't being told the whole truth. 'What else might 'one' say?'

'One might conclude sir, that the former Ambassador was perhaps... not a well person.'

'I see,' replied Kit again, hoping that he really did this time. 'Poor man – was it a man? It might just as well have been a woman; why not? I have not been given all the facts on this job and I have to tell you that it is making things very difficult. Kindly give me those facts now so that we can all get on with representing our country in a way which brings credit to it and be done with this muddley mess.'

Archibald Grant, to his credit did just that, though it was not a happy story.

The previous ambassador had indeed been a man, one Sir Percival Percy, a highly educated man who, like Kit, had won promotion in the Foreign Office, working his way up through the ranks with both speed and honour. He had mastered several languages, successfully negotiated a number of trade and peace deals around the world, been captured by bandits more than once, and finally been taken hostage in some far-flung country where he was accused of being a spy and had lived on bread and water for exactly two hundred and twelve days. Eventually, he had been released to international acclaim, but was a shadow of his former self. Not only had he survived somehow, but he had also written a bestseller about his awful escapades. His assignment in Carletia had provided an opportunity to serve somewhere less volatile, to keep his mind busy and his body nourished, and great things were expected of him. However, the powers that be had failed to take into account the long-term effects of some of the man's more traumatic experiences, which began to make themselves known almost as soon as he arrived in Carletia.

'This is dreadful!' exclaimed Kit. 'What on earth happened to the poor chap?'

Archibald Grant rubbed the side of his nose thoughtfully.

work, more distant from the staff here. He often shut himself in his room and began to miss meetings with governmental delegations in Carletia too.'

'So what did you do?' Kit enquired.

'Well, we all thought it was just a phase to be honest Sir, so we bluffed for a while. Various ministers, secretaries and counsellors stood in for him in meetings and we bumped along fairly well for a while. No one seemed to notice too much, and although we requested an assessment from London, and perhaps a new appointment, no one at home replied; so we just carried on as best we could. But then, recently, things got worse.'

Mr. Grant looked embarrassed and took an imaginary piece of fluff from his suit. It seemed that he didn't want to look his boss in the eye.

'Go on,' Kit urged; he was intrigued by this strange tale.

'Sir Percival spent more and more time locked in his room. He would appear from time to time looking dishevelled and unkempt.'

'Unkempt?'

No one was unkempt in the RAF; sharp seams and smartness were the required order of the day, along with regular haircuts and vigorous boot polishing. Kit Armitage would have no truck with unkemptness.

'Indeed, Sir. I'm sorry to say that he neglected his personal hygiene to the point that things became quite impossible.' Mr. Grant wrinkled his nose in distaste to demonstrate the point. 'It was better when he was outside in the fresh air, but he just couldn't concentrate. He would drift off during meetings – go blank – eventually it was as if he couldn't hear us anymore. He would sit for hours on a bench or in a deckchair, as still as a statue. He liked to feed the birds, but they began to start making nests in his hair – pecking his skin, shedding feathers, that sort of thing. Things just went from bad to worse. And then, last year they went way beyond awkward.'

'Awkward? What do you mean?'

'Well, we finally managed to get him out of his room for a social gathering. We changed the locks then, keeping the keys ourselves so he couldn't shut himself in there again. The Embassy was due to host a gala dinner for the President of Carletia; it's an annual affair and until now we've got away with it, you know – made excuses for Sir Percival. We said he was ill, or been delayed on a foreign mission, or recalled for a briefing; all sorts of schemes to cover up the truth. Unfortunately, a fortnight before the Gala, we lost him. He literally slipped through our fingers as some of the staff tried to force him into a bath. Perhaps it wasn't the best plan, but he just disappeared; we couldn't find him anywhere. Of course, we sent more urgent messages home but still no reply, so we had to just keep calm and carry on really.'

Archibald Grant allowed himself a smile at his feeble attempt at humour. The new Ambassador to Carletia ignored this and gestured that he should continue.

'The evening always ends with fireworks, or a band or something, so the President and dignitaries went out onto the terrace for the usual finale. Well sir, there was Sir Percival wearing nothing but his birthday suit, up to his knees in the ornamental fountain, splashing around and covered with birds.'

Mr. Grant shuddered as he recalled the humiliating evening.

'Good gracious!'

'Exactly, Sir. It was seen as a great insult to the President; he took it all rather personally I'm afraid. He and his entourage left immediately, expressing their horror and vowing never to return. There was a national outcry. The newspaper headlines were shocking; we just couldn't cover it up anymore. When word reached London they were on the phone immediately. I stood in for a while doing my best but it was uphill work. We were all very relieved when some months later, you arrived.'

'I'm so sorry Mr. Grant. That must have been very difficult for you all. And Sir Percival?'

'A team were sent here directly sir; medics, carers and the like, who managed to assess the ambassador and take him back to England, where I understand he is getting the help and care he has needed for some time.'

'Poor man,' murmured Kit, 'what a terrible thing for him; especially after coming through so many ordeals in the past. He must have been haunted by them.'

'Exactly sir,' Mr. Grant affirmed, 'he never really recovered from that last situation by all accounts.'

He heaved a sigh which suggested relief as well as concern for his former boss.

'It does put you in rather a tight spot though, sir.'

'How so?'

'Well,' Mr. Grant cleared his throat apologetically, 'that was a year ago, which means that the next Annual Gala Dinner is actually scheduled for Thursday.'

Kit looked up in alarm.

'This Thursday?!!! But that's not possible. I mean, if things between our two countries are still unresolved and tensions are running so high, we need to fix this. Immediately.'

'Yes, sir,' agreed Mr. Grant, 'we most definitely do.'

Kit began to pace up and down in agitation, stroking the back of his head repetitively – an action that indicated deep thinking on his part. He stopped abruptly and turned to his second-in-command.

'Why didn't I know about this before? It's a catastrophe waiting to happen. This is quite absurd!'

'It does rather seem that way, Sir,' agreed Mr. Grant. 'I fear that particular file may have not received your attention yet?'

This was true; it had originally been at the top of the pile and was even marked, *Urgent*; but when an over enthusiastic cleaner had accidentally sent the whole lot tumbling from the desk, she hadn't been able to remember which order they were in. Being in a rush, she simply rearranged them randomly and hoped for the best.

'Would you allow me?' asked Mr. Grant before thumbing through the rather stuffed 'in' tray that was still awaiting Kit. He gently wriggled out an orange file from the bottom of the pile.

'As I thought,' he said ruefully, placing it in front of his horrified boss. 'I'm sure you will come up with something, sir. I understand the RAF are very good at planning and making decisions under pressure. In fact, I believe that's one of the reasons why you were specifically chosen for the job, Sir. Unfortunately, you should also be aware that our budget for this event has been slashed drastically this year.'

Mr. Grant extracted a piece of paper from the file which showed most definite signs of mice nibbling round the edges, and brought it to the desk where Kit Armitage now sat in deep thought stoking the back of his head with some force.

'We will be operating on a shoestring, I'm afraid,' Mr. Grant informed the Ambassador. 'Really, very little to speak of on the financial front. I'll check in with you tomorrow if that's all right with you sir.'

Kit nodded and slumped into a chair, his head in his hands but his mind now racing.

True to his well-deserved reputation for calmness under pressure, he didn't waver, but began the challenging task before him. Plans needed to be made, menus must be devised, entertainment must be booked, all on a scale which would win back the favour of the Carletian government and erase the memories and unfortunate outcome of last year's disastrous Gala Dinner; and all by Thursday.

They barely had three days; it was a tall order for anyone.

Tuesday morning saw a whirlwind of activities as Kit Armitage, smart as ever, crammed himself into a pair of overalls and began a systematic search of the entire establishment. Taking his chargé d'affaires with him, the two men opened cupboards, looked under beds, turned out drawers and ransacked the garden shed, finding all sorts of surprising things along the way. Mr. Grant was less surprised. One time he had found all the official embassy cutlery at the bottom of the swimming pool and, on another occasion, the entire contents of the Ambassador's wardrobe strung up in the orchard like bunting. Sir Percival really had been a very ill man, and his brain had become so confused that his behaviour had become equally erratic.

Up in the attic there was a treasure trove of jumble, including a pile of old typewriters and some stuffed beavers (you may not know this, but Carletia is known for its flourishing beaver population. In fact, they are the national animal and feature prominently on their coat of arms). Coat cupboards which could no longer be used because they were full of old curtains (the Ambassador's residence boasted some rather nice, modern, hand-made wooden blinds these days) were investigated. There were boxes filled with old polaroid cameras; shelves jammed with toppling piles of ancient telephone directories from years ago; cases with odd collections of unidentifiable bits and bobs; rusty car parts; ancient nightlights; wonky umbrellas; dusty folding chairs – some broken; tins of paint; fishing rods; boxes of sad looking musical instruments, and several bags of old Christmas decorations all rather the worse for wear.

'Do you think we should be doing a bit more planning?' enquired Archibald Grant holding up an old step ladder and consequently dislodging a set of golf clubs which landed on his toe causing him considerable pain.

'This... is... planning,' grunted Kit, shoving a disintegrating cat basket back into the storeroom and tugging a sad-looking barbecue out from under a moulting rug. 'You told me yourself that we have to do this thing on a shoestring budget, so we're going to need to recycle some things.'

Mr. Grant looked at their findings somewhat doubtfully, but said nothing.

They both emerged from the stuffy space shaking dust from their hair, and coughing profusely. With twenty years worth of debris packed into every available storage space, it took the men some time to work their way through everything and collapse, exhausted, back in Kit's office.

'I'm not entirely sure how any of this will help us,' Mr. Grant finally confessed as he sipped some welcome coffee which had arrived long after the usual elevenses time.

'Neither am I, to be honest,' admitted Kit, 'but I had to see what we're working with.'

He drew a sheet of paper towards himself.

'I read through your files yesterday and made a list of some of the things the gala has done in the past in order to choose what we do this year.'

He scanned the list and handed it over to be scrutinised by his helper. Archibald Grant read the list quietly and with growing unease. It included a marching band, an aeronautic fly-by, a military display, an eight-course banquet, a string quartet, a laser show, a display of horse-riding, a world-class magician… the list went on and on with extravagant and extraordinary possibilities, none of which they could possibly provide without a lot of hard cash, which they didn't have, and with only two days to go.

Drawing on all his RAF experience, Kit Armitage knew that when the chips are down it's time for the heroes to stand up. He was well aware that the list was ambitious; he had merely itemised events from previous years. Considering that poor Sir Percival Percey had been rather ill for a jolly long time, it was amazing that any gala dinners had been able to take place at all. In fact, it was a testament to the teamwork and hard slog of the people who worked there, all of whom were now totally exhausted by having kept up the illusion of efficiency when really, things had been falling apart.

Kit consulted the list.

'I'm delegating a few things to you for the rest of the morning. You need to get our military contingent spruced up, practised and ready to perform marching manoeuvres in formation. I need the aeronautic display team here pronto, a representative of the Carletia Philharmonic Orchestra here for 2pm and a caterer here by 3pm to plan a menu. I will crack on with some of the other jobs.'

The two men parted, each aware that there was an awful lot to do, and it wasn't even lunch time.

Archibald Grant wished it were lunchtime, or preferably lunchtime in a fortnight when all this would be long over. When lunchtime did eventually roll around, he had had no luck with any of the tasks he had been assigned and reluctantly phoned through to the Ambassador's office where the phone was snatched up almost immediately.

'Ah, Mr. Grant; I was rather hoping you were the Carletia National Guild of Polka Dancers.' Kit's voice came through with ill-disguised disappointment.

'Sorry to let you down there, Sir,' Mr. Grant apologised; 'just me I'm afraid, and quite a lot of bad news.'

He wasn't exaggerating.

The military contingent were apparently away on exercise ten days sail from Carletia, so could not possibly be back by Thursday. The aeronautical display crew were on a team building exercise and silent retreat, so they could not be contacted. The entire Philharmonic Orchestra was down and out with a virulent bout of food poisoning, and the National Union of Caterers were currently on strike, wrangling with the government over higher pay and better chef hats.

'Not much luck here either,' Kit confessed. 'We can't have a light and laser show as there's a power cut scheduled for the entire day while the national grid gets a revamp, apparently.'

A secretary knocked and came in with a note bearing more bad news. The Carletia National Guild of Polka Dancers were way on a national tour of the Faroe Islands and consequently, quite out of reach.

The gentlemen couldn't have had worse luck in their attempts to get organised. Now it was back to the drawing board.

'I'm sorry you gentlemen have had such a tough day,' observed Mrs. Blantyre, the housekeeper, as she oversaw supper that night. 'I hear you're in rather a pickle.'

The men could only agree.

'I do wish you'd let us help you.'

'Thank you Mrs. Blantyre, I appreciate that,' sighed Kit, 'though I'm not sure how you can, unless you can magic up some ideas for us.'

'Well, I do think your recycling idea was a good one, sir. I couldn't help noticing that you'd turned everything out today.'

That was an understatement. Mrs. Blantyre had had reports that several chambermaids had tripped over old curtains left on the landing – one had twisted her ankle quite badly and was still sitting with it strapped up and iced. She had had to pick her own way through various obstacles left strewn indiscriminately across the corridors.

Kit had been so busy on the phone that he'd almost forgotten the activity of the morning, but once reminded by Mrs. Blantyre, he knew she was absolutely right. They had no other resources except what was under their own roof so, by golly, they would use it – every last piece, if Kit could find a role for it.

With a new resolve in his eye, the Ambassador pushed aside the remains of his cherry pie and custard, rubbed his hands together and stood up.

'You're right, Mrs. Blantyre. Where there's a will there's a way. Where there's a pile of old stuff, there's also treasure and possibility. Let's go!'

He strode purposefully from the room, and before long the staff were recalled to join him on the main landing. They were keen to help – after all, the reputation of the Embassy and the nation was at stake. Some came from their gym classes, some from their supper and several came in their rumpled pyjamas and dressing gowns. In this hour of crisis, it didn't matter at all, not even to Kit Armitage who still ironed creases into his own pyjamas.

All his years in the RAF, flying planes, training men, strategising and navigating sticky situations came back to Kit in a rush. His tiredness fell away and a new surge of energy pulsed through his veins as he gave orders, assigned tasks and discussed possibilities.

Before long, people were running here and there gathering all the detritus of the morning's discoveries. There was a buzz of activity which went on through the night, all the next day and into the Wednesday evening. Fires were lit, sewing machines hummed, shredders shredded, and people knuckled down to the immensity of their new jobs. They cat-napped when they could; Mrs. Blantyre furnished everyone with endless supplies of tea and cheese toasties, and little by little progress was made on this ambitious project.

Thursday morning dawned all too soon. Several of the staff opted for a cold shower to wake themselves up, and tea drinkers switched to coffee in a bid to be alert for the rigours of the day. There was still lots to be done before the Gala Dinner; a few things to be practised and some tables and chairs to set up.

At 6pm, Kit Armitage stood on the darkening terrace, slightly nervous but assured he was certainly going to give the President of Carletia something different this year. He surveyed the tables and chairs on the lawn, cleaned and repaired; each sporting a nightlight and topped by a sunshade freshly painted with the familiar red white and blue of the Union Jack. The staff were getting changed by torchlight, and the kitchen was bustling despite the lack of electricity.

Mr. Grant emerged through the double doors, an expression of profound anxiety etched on his face.

'Mr. Armitage, Sir.'

'Come and see this splendid arrangement,' Kit called. 'No one will be able to tell it's all recycled once the sun has gone down.'

'But he's not coming, sir.'

'What?'

'Remember, he said he wouldn't darken our doors again after last year's disaster? We forgot. We've just had word from his Chief of Staff: he's not coming.'

Kit was thunderstruck. This was catastrophic indeed. He felt his heart sink for a good twenty seconds. How could he have forgotten such an important detail? All their efforts would be for nothing if the guest of honour failed to show up. The stiff breeze had become a definite wind now, and was playing havoc with the tablecloths. Kit took a deep breath, pulled his shoulders straight and turned to Mr. Grant.

'In that case, we must go to him.'

Leaving a skeleton staff behind, the entire British Embassy assembled in the hall for new instructions. It was quite a sight, not least because everyone was wearing new uniforms, and very smart they looked too. The resilient and adaptable men and women who were employed by the British Government in Carletia were not necessarily military people themselves, but their new outfits matched beautifully. They had been artfully made from the stash of old curtains and trimmed with ribbons removed from the pile of ancient typewriters. Each sported a newly minted commemorative medal made from the melted down typewriters themselves, and imprinted with both the date and the face of the Carletian President copied from local currency.

Setting off up the dark and blustery drive of the British Embassy, they marched in step down the main city road to the President's house. Several vans followed them loaded with equipment for the evening's new schedule. Kit, resplendent in his RAF uniform led the way carrying a freshly cleaned stuffed beaver as both mascot and peace offering. He led his staff through the iron gates and into the ornamental gardens to the President's house where they stopped.

Kit turned to face his wonderfully supportive staff, and gave a signal as Mr. Grant rang the doorbell. The front door opened and, lit by the headlights of the vans, the ensemble lifted something to their mouths and blew.

The unmistakable melody of the Carletian national anthem filled the air. The effect was startling; a sound which finally drew even the curious, but severe, Carletian President out of his home and onto the porch. As you will know, anyone can play a kazoo – for that is what each musician had in their curtain-pockets – you don't need to be able to read music, you just hum into it. They are also very cheap to buy. Perfect.

Kit moved forward, greeted the guest of honour and offered him both a hand shake and his gift of the stuffed beaver. Such was the culture of Carletia, that the President could not possibly refuse such a gift. Now his hands were free, Kit drew from his pocket a shiny box which had once held Christmas baubles. Opening it, Kit presented the most important man in Carletia with a larger version of one of the newly minted commemorative medals. The President, who had seemed so stiff and full of the offences of the past, visibly relaxed and stroked his substantial moustache as, astonished and flattered, he recognised his own whiskered features on the medal.

As the newly formed kazoo orchestra battled with the increasingly mischievous wind, they moved on to playing a section of local folk songs, and Kit pinned the medal onto the President's lapel.

At that moment two other things happened: the van drivers, now atop their vehicles, threw the contents of large sacks into the air and a rain of ticker tape came fluttering down like confetti. The shredded telephone directories were a perfect substitute for the real thing. The paper snow was joined by glittering Christmas decorations which sparkled in the headlights, attached to fishing rods wielded by other staff. The whole effect was quite beautiful.

The official handshake was repeated with genuine warmth as the musicians crescendoed with a rousing rendition of the British National Anthem. All, it seemed might be forgiven and forgotten in the light of this marvellous show of international affection.

And now, although there was no eight-course banquet, a totally unplanned grand finale began. As the crowd of people stood on the President's driveway, Union Jacks began to flutter down across his garden, some bearing frightened waiters and waitresses.

Kit was as astonished as the man on whose lawn he stood.

The extraordinarily high winds had plucked the parasols from the Embassy garden and whooshed them over the treetops, where they landed perfectly (fortunately, no one was speared by the spiky shafts) amongst the ornamental flowerbeds. The effect was spectacular and the Carletian President, in spite of himself, began to clap energetically. Kit could not have planned for anything better.

Then, with impeccable timing, the electricity suddenly came back on making everybody squint in the glare of illumination. There were enthusiastic cheers of both relief and adulation. Mrs. Blantyre bustled around with one of the old cameras taking instant photographs to record the event – of course no one had been able to charge their phone all day and she had been commissioned to present the Carletian President with an album of photographs before the evening was over.

'Mr President, sir,' began the King's newest ambassador, 'I hope you will forgive our intrusion and the rather unorthodox display for this year's Gala Dinner. We would have hated for you to miss it and we wanted you to know how much we esteem and honour you, and your country, who so generously host us as representatives of our own country, throughout the year. My name is Kit Armitage and I am the new Ambassador here.' He gave a little bow which he certainly hadn't learned in the RAF.

The President smiled and looked down at his new medal.

'A new day, I think, perhaps,' the Carletian President said graciously, making an expansive gesture to the rag-tag orchestra and the wind-blown staff. 'This is certainly a little different this year.'

'Yes, indeed,' Kit agreed. 'We have adapted somewhat to the unusual circumstances…'

'I see you have been very enterprising. What is this that I am now smelling?'

'It's supper, sir,' Kit announced, indicating the area now cleared of kazoo players where barbecues had been fired up and large tureens were bubbling away.

Certainly not an eight-course banquet – this was supper with a distinct cultural difference. With practically no money to spend on a formal feast, Kit had worked with the kitchen to conjure up some good old British beans on toast. Mr. Grant was currently engaged in toasting bread on one grill, while the baked beans heated in huge cauldrons on another. (He had, of course, begun with some butter in his pan, which is how the best and tastiest baked beans are always cooked. You must try it for yourself if you haven't already done so.)

With an impressive slickness and efficiency, the tables and chairs from the Embassy were re-erected around the garden, and the President of Carletia sat down to the most memorable Gala Dinner he had ever had the good fortune to attend. Good relations had been resumed at last.

Back in London they heaved a collective sigh of relief when an urgent, if abrupt, message from Carletia came through to the Prime Minister via the foreign Office:

Diplomacy restored. Annual Gala Dinner success.

Beaver presented. Back on track.

Normal relations re-instituted.

Kazoos available for other diplomatic events

on request

Kit Armitage, ex-RAF, Ambassador to Carletia, and recycler extraordinaire had not only saved the day (again), but achieved what the British Prime Minister had secretly thought quite impossible. Back in the book-lined office at Downing Street, the PM cleaned his glasses on today's silk handkerchief, and inked up a stamp he very seldom got to use. Reaching for the original commissioning file he had given Kit, he thumped it down onto the cover, leaving an imprint in large red letters of the pleasing words: *MISSION ACCOMPLISHED*.

He congratulated himself on the genius idea of appointing Kit in the first place, wished he had more such brilliant ideas, and went in search of a celebratory cup of cocoa while remembering the old, red kazoo he had once found in his Christmas stocking, as a child.

The Beasley-Babbingtons

The house was a death-trap.

There was no denying it, the whole colossal crumbling castle was pretty much falling down.

Baxter Beasley-Babbington surveyed the ancient family home from the gravel drive. If he screwed up his eyes, put his head on one side and if the daylight was fading, then it still looked pretty impressive. However, he couldn't stand like that all day without getting a crick in his neck, and neither could anyone else.

The walkie-talkie in his hand buzzed into life as his brother's voice came through, sounding as though he was calling from Nova Scotia rather than from inside the old house.

'It's a no-go here. Over,' crackled the voice of Bartholomew.

'What can you see?' asked Baxter.

'You didn't say, 'Over.' Over,' came the reply.

Baxter Beasley-Babbington rolled his eyes, although there was no one to see him. His brother was always such a stickler for protocols.

'Question remains: what can you see? *Ov-er*.' He emphasised the last word in an effort to communicate his irritation.

'Right now, I can see daylight. There are holes in the roof and I've just ruined my shoes walking through the puddles on the landing. Everything in the attic is probably ruined. You could say it's 'Over'.'

Bartholomew's chortle crackled over the airways while more eye-rolling took place at ground level.

'You'd better come down. Over.'

'Right-o. Might be tricky though; most of the stairs are gone. It's a miracle I got up this far. Over and out.'

Baxter Beasley-Babbington sighed more heavily than his doctor would have thought advisable, and crunched his way towards the front door where he waited for his brother to appear. On closer inspection, the brass door knocker was hanging crookedly, the entire oak structure looked as though it was being eaten by woodworms, and the letter box was long gone.

You may wonder why such a large family home had come into such a desperate state of disrepair. The Beasley-Babbington brothers certainly did.

They came from an old family who, many years ago had occupied the vast building along with a swarm of chambermaids, butlers, valets, and housekeepers during an age when the wealthy members of the nation ran their estates for the local towns and villages, providing jobs for huge numbers of people. From their extensive grounds, crops were cultivated so people were fed, employed and integrated into lively communities who marked the cycle of seasons in traditional ways with feasts or dances, fairs, or outings to the seaside. Perhaps that doesn't sound very exciting to you, but a hundred and fifty years ago all those things were anticipated with great excitement and savoured for weeks afterwards.

However, times changed, as they always do. No one needs to live in such a massive mansion anymore – just think of the heating bills. All the staff had moved on or retired years ago, leaving one spinster aunt to struggle on in Babbington Castle. Both Baxter and Bartholomew remembered Great-Aunt Matilda as being ancient when they were still little boys, so goodness know how old she had been when she finally passed away. Now, the government wanted money from the estate and the boys – now grown men – had a castle on their hands with neither plan nor idea about what to do with it, and a massive tax bill.

'It's too bad,' complained Baxter over a fortifying cup of tea poured from a tartan-patterned flask, as he sat next to his brother in the car some time later.

Bartholomew was concentrating on spooning vast quantities of sugar into his cup without spilling it all over the floor. His tongue was clamped firmly between his lips as he did so, reminding Baxter of their father, who had done exactly the same thing whenever he was trying to focus on a project. Bartholomew grunted noncommittally.

'Really, Father should have sorted this out long ago. It's ridiculous that Great-Aunt Matilda lived there all this time. I had no idea things were so bad.'

This was true. They were not mean brothers. They simply had not realised that their great-aunt had been living in such terrible conditions for so long. Being rather eccentric, she had not really noticed how decrepit everything was either. Her memory was failing and having lived through two world wars, she was used to going without, and making do. As her health deteriorated, she slept a lot and her mind took her back to the days when she was a young girl. So, when no one came to help her or visit her, she assumed they'd all gone out for the day and didn't think to find someone who could change things. She'd always been suspicious of the telephone and avoided using it. Truth to tell, the mice had long since chewed through every wire and cord in the house, so she couldn't have reached the boys if she'd wanted to. She'd never even heard of mobile phones. So, she'd eked out her existence living on the tinned goods that had been stored in piles from the second world war: mostly apricots and corned beef. Not an exciting diet, but she wasn't bothered about that.

What I haven't told you, is that until very recently, the brothers had both been abroad working for an international finance company, and had assumed that various cleaning ladies and local services had been looking after their poor aunt. They had been summoned back to England by a legal letter which named them as joint heirs of the family pile; hence their dismal visit today.

Bartholomew completed his sugar gymnastics and was stirring his tea thoughtfully.

'Good job Belinda hasn't seen it. Our sister would have a fit. What happens next? We shall have to sell, I suppose,' he pondered ruefully.

'Well, I don't think we can *live* there,' answered his brother. 'I know *I* don't want to,' he added emphatically. 'Do you?'

Bartholomew groaned. 'It doesn't seem terribly practical right now, I must say. Pity though. Lots of good memories from here. I was rather hoping to come home and retire.'

'Nonsense,' snorted his brother scornfully. He was already thumbing through the local paper to find a number for a local estate agent. 'We must get it valued immediately.'

Pulling out his mobile phone, he began jabbing at the numbers. Bartholomew groaned again. 'Where is Belinda these days, anyway?'

'Last I heard she was on some retreat in Patagonia learning how to make indigenous plants into natural remedies. She's miles from civilisation, so no help to us whatsoever, and completely unreachable.'

Bartholomew sighed almost as heavily as his brother had done.

'Chin up, Barty,' Baxter said, trying to lift the mood. 'Let's gather the information before we make any decisions. I vote we stay at that nice little guest house we passed on the way in, until we get this sorted out.'

With that Bartholomew had to be satisfied, and he prudently buried his disappointment in the paper which he had retrieved from his brother, where he began to read the letters page – often the most informative section of any local publication.

A couple of days later the brothers could be seen on another visit, joined by a tall, thin gentleman in a large raincoat which hung from his shoulders reminding the brothers of a bedraggled vulture they'd once seen on a rainy day at the zoo. His droopy moustache gave off the air of one consistently disappointed by life, and he had a terrible habit of sniffing with every disparaging remark.

'Oh dear me,' he said, as soon as he unfolded himself from a small maroon coloured car. He gave a false laugh which was as thin as he was.

'Oh dear, dear me; what have we *here*?' He cast his eyes swiftly over the once proud castle and surrounding acres and sniggered nastily.

The brothers frowned at one another. This was not what they were expecting.

Baxter stepped up: 'Ah, Mr. Melrose? We spoke on the phone, I believe. I'm Baxter Beasley-Babbington and this,' he indicated Bartholomew standing miserably beside him, 'is my brother.'

'Delighted,' Mr. Melrose said in an oily voice which indicated anything but delight. He winced as his damp, limp hand was given a firm shake by each of the brothers who had been brought up to know that such a gesture indicates both good manners and confidence.

'Shall we begin the tour?' added Baxter with an attempt at good humour.

'Well,' Mr. Melrose dripped on; 'I'm not sure it will make much difference,' he sniffed heartily; 'but I suppose that's why you asked me here.'

So saying he stepped disdainfully over a shattered, leaded window and, taking out a clipboard and pen from a vast pocket inside his oversized coat, he began his appraisal of the castle.

They moved from room to room: the hallway, the morning room, the dining room, the study, the drawing room, the withdrawing room, the library, the ballroom and a sad collection of other rooms that had once been the kitchen, pantry, scullery and store rooms. In every one, Mr. Melrose, drew his breath in through his teeth with a hiss of loathing, tutted to himself, sniffed in disapproval and scribbled spidery notes on his pad.

He lifted the carpets to look at the floorboards, prodded peeling wallpaper, pulled wonky doors off their hinges, poked at window fittings, tapped walls, observed the faded rectangles where paintings had once hung, and screwed up his eyes to survey the ceilings – in places where there were any ceilings left. All the time, he whispered and laughed to himself, ignoring the two men who remembered the house as a place of warmth and childhood joy.

To say he was insensitive is an understatement. Great Aunt Matilda would have told Mr. Melrose off quite soundly for being so rude, and she would certainly have recommended a handkerchief for that infernal sniffing.

Finally, having picked his way up the backstairs, which were marginally more solid than the main staircase, Mr. Melrose examined what was left of the bedrooms. More sniggering and more sniffing, followed by more note-taking.

'Of course, it all needs pulling down really,' he commented between sniffs. 'Needs rewiring, reglazing, repointing – ha! Rebuilding really...'.

The brothers could see all this for themselves, as you would have done too had you been there. Mr. Melrose was not telling them anything they didn't already know.

'People want en-suites these days,' he went on. 'No one wants this sort of thing at all. Dear me, no. Quite unsuitable. Too many stairs. Not

enough stairs. Florals are out too, of course. People are looking for cosy, easy to run, cheap-to-heat apartments. Bit of a blow for anyone harking back to being lord-of-the-manor.' Here he gave an enormous sniff and threw a scornful but meaningful glance at the brothers. ''Course, you'd need a modern lift to access all floors. Ever thought of that? Your roof is nothing short of shocking. I assume there are no fire regs operating currently?'

Baxter and Bartholomew both thought this was a pretty stupid question given that the castle was currently little more than a ruin.

'No?' Mr. Melrose ploughed on. 'As I thought.'

He sniffed again; this time so hard he made his own head hurt and his ears popped with the pressure, making his eyes water briefly.

'Those attics… tut, tut. I haven't come across anything this horrible for a number of years. Dear me, no. No; it's all a *mess* gentlemen.' He clicked his tongue as he assessed his findings. 'You'd need a plumber, new hot and cold tanks, new roof, new walls and doors, obviously, complete rewiring. No one wants the sort of grounds you have here. Best to sell it all to a developer really; get it off your hands at the first opportunity would be my advice. All very horrible. Very unattractive. Very impractical. Good morning.'

With that, Mr. Melrose edged carefully back down the stairs, refolded himself into his little car and drove away, still sniffing and sniggering to himself.

The brothers were glum as they returned to their own car.

'What an unpleasant man,' observed Bartholomew.

'I can't argue with you there,' agreed Baxter.

'We didn't ask whether he *liked* it; we simply wanted a valuation.'

The brothers shook their heads and headed off to find consolation in lunch at a local restaurant. They knew, as I'm sure you do, that if you want the type of information they were looking for, you employ the services of more than one person. It's getting a second, or even a third opinion, which helps you gather really good information.

Consequently, the Beasley-Babbington brothers, fortified by mushroom soup and treacle tart (though not served in the same bowls), visited another estate agent themselves. Messrs Rawlings, Scaffold and Drew were much more professional and efficient. By the end of the week they had visited, assessed and drawn up a valuation, including suggestions for the way forward.

Like Mr. Melrose, they had suggested transforming the property into individual apartments, selling to a supermarket or donating the whole thing to *The National Heritage Society* who, in their considered opinion, might be open to such a gift, or have access to the vast sums of money required to restore it to its former glory. Their valuation, while reasonable and a considerable amount, would never cover the cost involved in repairing the family home once the government had received their substantial share.

The brothers scratched their heads, umm-ed, err-ed and shrugged their shoulders by turns. The way before them was anything but clear as they retreated once again to the guest house where their hostess, Mrs. Jackson, had made them welcome.

'Now then gents,' she said as she bustled about with a teapot, filling their cups for the third time that afternoon; 'there's always a solution. Just because you can't see it yet, doesn't mean it's not there. My old mother taught me that. These things are usually right under your nose if you only take the time to look.'

Baxter came very close to snorting into his hot tea at this point; he was tired, dispirited and found this kind of talk immensely irritating. Bartholomew, on the other hand, managed to be quite gracious.

'My dear Mrs. Jackson,' he began, 'I'm not quite sure what you can mean. Do you have some information which might help us with our plans?'

The lady in question looked somewhat uncomfortable, realising that she might have stepped beyond the bounds of politeness, and offended her guests.

'No not really Mr. Beasley-Babbington. I didn't mean to upset you gentlemen. Goodness knows, your family has been in this village far longer than mine. It's a question of modernising really though, isn't it?'

She put her head on one side in much the same way that Baxter had done that first day they had visited the castle. 'Perhaps the idea of apartments isn't so bad, but it would change the village enormously. I don't think people would like that.'

'Really?' observed Baxter, drily. 'I thought change was the only thing that ever stayed the same.'

Mrs. Jackson frowned as she tried to work out whether that was a joke or whether the elder

Mr. Beasley-Babbington had just said something very wise. She wasn't at all sure which it was. She shuffled nervously and wrapped her hands more tightly round the teapot.

'I'm sure you clever gentlemen will come up with something. It's just that a supermarket would mean more traffic wouldn't it? Very useful in some respects – save me trekking off on the bus every week for a start – but there's the parking isn't there? All those beautiful grounds buried under concrete and tarmac. It would be a real shame; doesn't seem quite right.'

Neither Baxter nor Bartholomew could disagree with Mrs. Jackson on that point. Bartholomew had been pondering the idea of a wedding venue. He'd seen an advert for one some distance away in the local paper, and had overheard someone at lunch bemoaning the fact that so many places were booked up years in advance. Apparently, securing a booking was terribly difficult.

Baxter was having none of it.

'No, no,' he dismissed his brother's new idea with a wave of his hand; 'we're missing something here, I'm sure of it. I just can't think what it is.'

Several sleepless nights followed, as the brothers grappled with anxiety and stared into the darkness hoping for inspiration. They had received another letter from the solicitors written in both capital letters and an eye-watering quantity of red ink, which put the fear of God into them. It demanded payment of what they owed within a horrifically short period of time.

During daylight hours, they waded through ideas, googled their questions on a battered laptop and even went to the local council offices to research other developments in the area. Baxter was determined to do something that would stand out; Bartholomew just wanted the whole ghastly situation resolved so he could have a full night of sleep again. Despite all their experience working in international finance, owing so much money made both of them feel rather wobbly; it was a huge sum after all.

Reluctantly, they had employed a firm to remove every last piece of dilapidated furniture from the castle, and clear the attics of boxes and trunks, in order to sell off the contents. They didn't have the heart to pick through everything themselves; much of it was ruined anyway. The sad collection of items languished in the county auction rooms until the monthly sales day, when prospective buyers flocked to find bargains for their own homes or, more frequently, for the businesses they ran themselves. Inspired by popular television programmes, people were always looking for old treasures in some shape or form which they could repair or upcycle, and sell on at a hefty profit.

On the morning of the auction itself, Bartholomew was crunching toast and marmalade while Baxter made short work of bacon and eggs. Leaving the local newspaper, in which he had been engrossed again, Bartholomew went upstairs to fetch his coat while Baxter glanced over at the open page. It seemed there was a lively exchange of letters going on regarding the recreational facilities in the area. Clearly people had very strong feelings on the matter. Baxter was glad it wasn't his problem. He wiped the remaining egg from his plate with a piece of bread – something else of which Great Aunt Matilda would not have approved – tossed his napkin onto the table and joined his brother in the hallway.

'Goodbye, Mrs. Jackson,' he called. 'We shall return once we have attended to our business in town.'

'Right you are, sir,' came the jaunty reply.

Parking was a nightmare, as it so often is, and the auction room was already buzzing with excitement when they arrived. With difficulty, the brothers found two seats next to each other and crossed their fingers, hoping that despite the soggy state of most of them, the items from Babbington Castle might bring in some serious money. They couldn't see as much as they'd hoped, thanks to the enormous hat being worn by a lady two rows in front of them. It had a wide brim and a large feather, which undulated in the breeze, blurring their view every time she moved her head.

Turning to the brochure they had been given, they were able to follow the progress of sales as items were displayed in turn. The auctioneer took bids from the floor and, occasionally, online, until he let his special hammer fall to mark that he had accepted the highest offer from the bidders. Their details were then written on an official form in front of him. The buyers all had a number marked on hand-held paddles which they could hold up to indicate they were raising the amount of money offered for something.

This is a very sensible way of doing things. Before such an arrangement people had accidentally purchased all manner of things they didn't want at all, simply by coughing at the wrong moment, sneezing in a way the auctioneer misinterpreted, or even absent-mindedly scratching their nose while looking out of the window. Many an innocent attendee had been compelled to go home with bits of old combine harvester, half a dozen military medals, or a set of ugly hand-painted vases, because they'd twitched at the wrong moment. Highly unsatisfactory, and often very embarrassing.

The brothers, of course, were here to watch, not to buy. They were trying to get rid of stuff, not accumulate more, so kept their numbered paddles firmly on their laps. The bidding was lively and the auctioneer didn't waste any time. He had a large number of 'lots' (as they are called) to get through, and an appointment with his middle son's chemistry teacher for which he didn't want to be late. Goodness knows what young Harry had been up to now, but his father intended to find out.

It took the better part of the morning to race through the content of the attics. A couple of trunks and a Persian rug in reasonable condition had aroused a good bit of interest, and the catalogue showed that they would be moving on to the furniture, such as it was, after lunch. Meanwhile, Baxter was interested to see that a stuffed pheasant was causing quite a stir in one corner of the auction house, where two gentlemen were raising both their voices and their bids in an effort to secure the (in his opinion) rather moth-eaten specimen.

Every now and again, this is what happens. A seller notices a trend for a style of item and realises that people will pay more to have such a thing displayed in their house. Somewhere in a corner of Suffolk, people were going mad for taxidermy – stuffed dead animals. Not the sort of thing I'd want in my house; I can't imagine you would want such a thing either, but there's no accounting for taste. There was an audible sigh of relief when the auctioneer's hammer came down as everyone relaxed and went, gratefully, to find some lunch.

Just as they were filing out, Baxter heard a voice calling him.

'I say, Baxter... Baxter... Baxter Beasley-Babbington!'

People turned to stare at such an unseemly outburst, as the woman in the large feathered hat emerged from the crowd to grasp Baxter's hands.

'Good gracious; Belinda!'

Belinda, for that is exactly who it was, laughed once at her brother's shocked face and laughed again as Bartholomew, who had also turned around, stared at her with amazement.

'Good heavens!' he echoed, 'Belinda!'

It's odd how people say the most obvious things when taken by surprise, or see something or someone familiar in a very unexpected place. The brothers were certainly surprised. Not just to see their sister in front of them when they had thought she was far away tracking rare plants in Patagonia, but by the extraordinary outfit she was wearing: a cross between a kaftan and a poncho in startling colours and topped by that very elegant, feathered hat which had been annoying them most of the morning. She looked rather like a character who has escaped from either a pantomime or a story book.

'What in heaven's name are you doing here?' said Bartholomew.

'I thought you were in Patagonia,' added Baxter, 'gathering plants or something…'

'Oh boys it's good to see you! Yes. I was; but a rather exciting thing has happened, and when I came back from the jungle to my hotel, I found a letter telling me Great-Aunt Matilda had died, and I must return at once. That's not exciting – obviously – it's very sad. I had no idea you would both be here until I saw the catalogue this morning full of items from the castle. I hoped you would turn up to watch.'

There was a hustle and bustle of greeting and some stiff hugging (the Beasley-Babbingtons had never been big huggers) as the siblings were reunited and managed to exit the building and settle in at the coffee shop opposite, for some welcome sustenance and to catch up on their respective news.

Here, the brothers explained how they had inherited the castle, and the sad state of disrepair into which it had fallen. Belinda nodded in the appropriate places, heard about the valuation, the horrendous tax bill and the limited options they felt were open to them, all while trying not to get her sleeves in the gravy.

'Do you want to do any of these things?' she asked when they'd finished their summation of them.

'Not at all,' moaned Bartholomew, pushing his fork disconsolately round his plate.

'Not really,' agreed Baxter, fiddling with his glass of water.

'Then let's do something else entirely!' There was a twinkle in their sister's eyes which the brothers knew from years ago meant that she already had a plan and they were about to be dragged into it.

'I didn't inherit the castle, so it's not my responsibility, but I did enjoy growing up there. What I did inherit was a rather fine painting that Great-Aunt Matilda inherited from her godfather ages ago, and which has been sitting safely in the vaults at Sothebys for a number of years.'

The brothers' eyebrows shot up immediately; they hadn't heard about this. They knew about Sothebys, of course: the famous auction house in London, but that their sister had a valuable painting? Not a whisper. Belinda laughed at them without malice.

'Well, dear old Aunty knew I wouldn't get a look in on the property what with all the stupid old-fashioned rules about male heirs – thank goodness those laws have changed now – so she decided to put that aside for me when I was about four-years-old. It's by some Dutch old master; terribly dark and not very interesting to look at. It's called something very dreary like *Woman tying her shoes*; I wouldn't give it houseroom myself. I like something with a bit of colour,' she waved her arms around to demonstrate. 'However, the clever Sotheby's chaps discovered that it was one of the artist's lost paintings, so it stirred up quite a lot of interest amongst collectors and turned out to be worth quite a bit of money.'

Belinda's brothers gawped at her in astonishment.

'We knew nothing about this,' gasped Baxter, trying to grasp what his sister was saying.

'Well of course not; why would you? It was mine and I made sure Sotheby's kept news of its discovery out of the limelight until the sale.'

'You've sold it already?' asked Bartholomew. 'We heard nothing; we've been abroad. Was it valued?

Is it insured? How much did it get? How is this possible?'

'Oh, pull yourself together,' scolded his sister. 'It's not a big deal. I'm sure the castle is worth something too.'

'Have you seen it recently?' enquired Bartholomew. 'It's not quite what it was.'

'He's not wrong,' agreed Baxter. 'Terrible state really.'

'Tut, tut,' Belinda clicked her tongue, reminding them for a fleeting moment of the unpleasant Mr. Melrose. 'You boys have no imagination; that's your problem. As a matter of fact, I went to look at the old pile as soon as I got back. It does look rather sorry for itself; but think what we could do with it.'

'Not much, according to the estate agents,' said Baxter forlornly. He counted off on his fingers: 'Apartments; supermarket; sell it to some historical chaps, seems to be about the size of it. Oh, and

Bartholomew through it might make good wedding venue.'

'Pah!' said Belinda, with feeling and a modicum of scorn.

'Rather a sad ending for such a lovely home,' agreed Bartholomew. He wondered at that moment whether perhaps he had something in his eye…

'We thought the auction might raise some money, but that tax bill is keeping us awake at night.'

Both brothers sighed heavily; it was becoming rather a habit. Belinda was having none of it.

'Nonsense; I can sort that out in a jiffy. You'd be amazed what collectors pay for old masters. They're welcome to it. It's the castle that we need to transform.'

It became clear that, just like her brothers, Belinda had no thought of living there herself, but she did have some other ambitious ideas. It also became clear that auctioning off the painting she'd inherited had made her enormously, stupendously wealthy. Baxter surreptitiously checked on line later and discovered a number with so many noughts, he had to count them twice. Belinda need never work again, except that she enjoyed her adventures in far flung places, and was disinclined to give them up.

Over and above all of this, was the news that Belinda had not only discovered rare plants which were of enormous interest to the *British Botanical Society*, but she had managed to develop entirely new strains which were far more suited to growing in the temporal climate of Great Britain than in the sultry jungles of Patagonia. And that was just part of the tale, for as she'd distilled and extracted juices from various hitherto unknown species, she'd developed a tincture which worked like a dream on bunions.

You don't know what bunions are, and I am not surprised. You are young enough to not be troubled by them. I can assure you that they are not a kind of exotic onion; neither are they those curious clips that are used on brand new shirts that come in packages from fancy shops; nor are they the horrible termites that eat your clothes. They are the bumps that develop, with age, in the joint where your big toe joins your foot; especially if you have worn shoes which are too tight for your toes – which is why you should always buy what your grandmother would call 'sensible' shoes. The pressure of tight shoes pushes your big toe towards the smaller ones and the bumpy bit can rub, and become very sore. Most older people suffer from them because they did not listen to their mothers and grand-mothers when purchasing footwear, so an ointment to relive the discomfort they cause is in great demand amongst the older generation in Europe and beyond.

Clever Belinda had found a product that would make her a fortune all over again, even without the sale of the inherited, *Woman tying her shoes* painting. She had already registered the idea so no one else could steal it, and designers were working on the packaging even as she sat with the brothers polishing off her excellent dessert.

She pushed her bowl aside and, before you could say 'rhubarb and custard', Belinda was sketching her ideas onto the tablecloth. Fortunately, it was a paper one which would otherwise have been thrown away. No linen was ruined by this activity; Great Aunt Matilda would have been mollified.

In front of their eyes the brothers saw a whole new idea coming to life, and they were astonished all over again.

'But this is amazing,' breathed Bartholomew in awe.

Belinda shrugged one shoulder as if to say, 'Of course.'

'Can we really pull this off?' asked Baxter reigning in his enthusiasm and bringing what he hoped was a bit of elder brother reality to proceedings.

'I don't see why not,' his sister replied. 'We have the funds, we have the village on our side – have you been following the letters page in the local paper? I've had it sent over to me for years to keep up with the news; it arrives a little late, of course, but it's amazing what an online subscription will do.'

'Of course!' exclaimed Bartholomew. 'Mrs. Jackson said it was right in front of us, if only we could see it.'

'But we couldn't,' acknowledged Baxter.

So it was that within the year, the gates and doors of Babbington Castle were opened to the good people of the town and beyond, who were all welcomed to the most wonderful enchanted gardens and forest designed by Belinda Beasley-Babbington, paid for by the sale of an obscure Dutch painting, and kept running from the profits of *Belinda's Brilliant Bunion Balm*, which was selling like hot cakes in every pharmacy on the continent, as well as online.

Here she could grow her hybrid plants without worrying that they might pick up some virulent tropical disease. The grounds were so large, that she was able to set up a developmental laboratory to find yet more uses for her wonderful plant cream. She mixed other combinations of exotic and local flora to target inconvenient and unpleasant conditions from which older people tend to suffer: chilblains, arthritis, rheumatism and wrinkles.

Her new blooms and extraordinary shrubs flourished throughout the grounds as well as inside the house.

The whole structure, though reinforced, was superbly open-plan allowing free movement between the garden and the house. The roof never was replaced with standard tiles either; there was no point. Instead, a beautiful spiral staircase took visitors up several storeys to explore a roof garden of such beauty that it often made them cry.

Best of all — at least, according to anyone under the age of ninety — was the introduction of a marvellous swimming pool. Not your standard leisure centre type of design, though. Belinda's pool was accessed by a fantastic assortment of slides of various heights and angles, all sprouting from a complex design of multiple stairways, which plunged into the welcoming water. This was heated by solar panels — quite a treat in chilly England, where outside pools are often shunned by those who prefer not to freeze or turn blue in the first three seconds of getting in.

Surrounding this fabulous recreational facility were equally fantastic plants. Belinda had cleverly incorporated leafy shrubs and towering trees into the whole complex, appealing to both adults and children alike.

Inspired by the towering flora she had encountered on her trips to Patagonia, Belinda had replicated as many as she could in the vast house space itself.

The rotten floors had been deconstructed and recycled, and the cellar lined and waterproofed to create this ingenious pool. What remained of the ballroom was made into changing rooms, heated by underground pipes, while the store rooms hosted a modest coffee shop. Everyone wants a hot drink after swimming regardless of the season, and this one served some of the most frothy and delicious hot chocolate you can imagine.

The whole village loved it; young and old alike. Mrs. Jackson was almost as delighted as the children.

'We've been telling the council for years that the recreational facilities were rubbish around here,' she told a reporter on the opening day, as she prepared to descend a twisty slide herself. 'There's been letters in the paper for as long as I can remember. It took all this time and a lot of imagination to come up with what the Beasley-Babbington's have designed. They've given us the most marvellous present. I think it's wonderful; I really do!'

And it was.

Baxter and Bartholomew still didn't want to live there; it had become rather a noisy place to be for extended periods of time, although the plants absorbed quite a lot of the shrieks and whoops of happy children and old age pensioners, several of whom found a new lease of life after a turn on the slides. Instead, they retired to a bungalow near Eastbourne and took to smoking pipes and reading piles of books. Baxter collected postcards, and Bartholomew took up bird-watching. I don't think that these are particularly exciting hobbies, and I am guessing that you don't either; but the brothers had had a lot of adventures in their former jobs and were content to now get their thrills by hearing about Belinda's latest adventures. There was no stopping her!

They'd recently received a postcard from her with a colourful picture of French Polynesia on the front. She reported that she'd just found a rare coral which she hoped might reinvigorate the dead corals off the coast of Australia, if only she could reproduce them.

In time, both Baxter and Bartholomew Beasley-Babbington believed she very probably would.

The Viticulture Venture

The Viticulture Venture

Shaun Scattergood let himself into the familiar house, kicked off his shoes, lent his skateboard against the old grandfather clock in the hallway, and replaced the key he'd just used back under the plant pot outside, being careful not to let the door shut again. It wasn't actually his house, but his Grandad – whose home it was – always left Shaun a hidden key because his own hearing wasn't what it used to be, so he didn't always hear the doorbell but he loved to have Shaun visit as often as he wanted. Shaun loved that too, partly because Grandad always had interesting snacks in his fridge, partly because it gave him an excuse not to go home where he would be asked to do all sorts of chores he didn't fancy doing, and partly because he loved his Grandad to bits, and enjoyed hearing his stories about growing up, and his tales of military life.

Grandad was a widower; Granny had been a lovely lady who smelt of lavender and made the most amazing roast potatoes, but she had died when Shaun was only five, so his memories of her were very hazy. It was obvious that Grandad missed her though, and he had taken up several hobbies to fill his retirement years. He grew vegetables, pottered in the greenhouse, and sometimes Shaun would help him plant out seedlings while hearing about exotic places he'd visited in his army days. Grandad had some shiny medals, tucked away carefully at the back of his sock drawer, which he sometimes let Shaun touch. They were very precious, and Grandad wore them with pride every year for the

Remembrance Day Parade to the war memorial in town.

Grandad had taken up bridge, which is a card game that old people seem to enjoy and which requires four players making up two teams of two. The local Bridge Club had welcomed their new member warmly. Shaun didn't really understand the game; it seemed rather complicated. Besides, he preferred careering around on his skateboard at the park, learning new tricks and practising his jumps with the other teenagers.

Grandad's other great interest was wine. You might think that's a very strange hobby; like saying that food is your hobby. Surely you just eat it or drink it? Well, funnily enough, people do collect wine that's made in different places and in different years. Real experts recognise variations in the taste, even if the winemaker uses the same type of grape. For example, one year there might have been a hot summer, or an unusually cold winter, which will affect the flavour of the wine. The older the wine, the more valuable it is. Some wines are sold at auction for hundreds, and even thousands, of pounds. There are bottles which have never actually been opened, because it would reduce their value – a bit like opening a box of chocolates and eating one and then trying to sell them to someone else. Yuk!

Grandad had travelled all over the world and had started collecting wine in his military days. He would bring back a bottle for Granny from Argentina, or France, or South Africa, or wherever he was stationed. Sometimes he chose a bottle because he liked the label or the name of the winery, or sometimes he might have had a glass of it somewhere with his friends on a day off. Granny hadn't really liked wine very much but thought it might look ungrateful if she told him so, since he'd made such an effort to find her a gift, and she thoroughly appreciated the thought.

After she had died, Grandad found the bottles gathering dust and lined up behind the wellies in the shed, behind the towels in the airing cupboard, and even behind the vegetable rack in the larder. Clever Granny; she had kept them all, knowing that one day they would be very valuable. Now Grandad kept them in his wonderful wine cellar on special racks – rows and rows of them – where he had once stored coal (there was no central heating when he first bought the house; it was rather an old house). No one was allowed to touch the bottles, except Grandad. There was even a padlock on the door; just in case.

Shaun didn't know anything about wine, except that you could get red or white made from different grapes. He was too young to be allowed to try it and he always thought it smelt funny anyway, so he stuck to fresh fruit juice. After all, if he was going to become a champion skateboarder he needed to be super strong, fit and healthy; and everyone knows that real sports professionals don't touch anything that will reduce their chances of winning. Right now he was hoping to find some guava juice in Grandad's fridge. He'd tried it last week and it had tasted delicious, even if it was rather pink. There was only standard apple juice in his fridge at home, which Shaun thought was really boring.

He wandered into the kitchen, calling for his Grandad as he went, but there was no answer. That was odd. He looked in the lounge, but Grandad wasn't there either. He wasn't in the dining room, the garden, the shed, the greenhouse, or the garage. Shaun went upstairs quietly, in case his grandfather had gone for a nap or was having a bath. Old people sometimes did things at funny times of day. Grandad sometimes ate breakfast at six in the evening and called it *brinner* – but he wasn't there either.

Oh well, thought Shaun, *he'll be back soon I expect. Maybe he's gone to the library, or is out playing cards with his friends.*

He found the juice, poured himself a glass and wandered around the kitchen flicking through a wine magazine left on the counter: *Viticulture Today*. It had some interesting pictures of lush vineyards in France and America; all the vines were growing in pleasing straight rows attached to trellises. Closing the magazine, Shaun moved on, passing the time by reading the flyers pinned next to Grandad's calendar on the wall, as he drank his juice. There was an invitation to someone's 90th birthday next week – yikes; that was old! But Shaun's eye was drawn to a photocopied invitation written by Grandad to The Bridge Club, inviting them all to a wine tasting at his house next week. He must have pinned an extra one there to remind himself. Shaun thought that was a good idea. Older people do begin to get rather forgetful, after all. It seemed that Grandad was actually planning to share some of his well-guarded wine. Shaun was surprised, but smiled to himself; Grandad was always so kind and had such creative ideas for activities. Last month he'd organised a skittles evening, and the month before that a trip to the zoo. Grandad would never be bored, that was for sure.

Shaun's thoughts were interrupted by a ring on the doorbell. He frowned. Who could that be? Grandad had his own key of course. Perhaps someone was delivering a parcel.

He put down his juice carefully, and went to answer just as the visitor leaned on the bell a second time.

'Humph! About time,' grunted the man on the doorstep as Shaun opened the door to discover four other grey-haired people behind him, all anxious to come in. He didn't have a chance to ask them who they were before they'd all bustled in, jostling past him – narrowly avoiding his skateboard –and into the dining room. Shaun closed the front door and hurried after them wondering not only who all these people were, but why old people wore so many clothes, even in summer. The visitors were settling themselves around the table, shaking off coats and hats.

The first man seemed to be the leader and rubbed his hands together expectantly.

'Right young man; I assume the Major will be joining us soon. You must be the sommelier today, what?!'

'I'm sorry, the what now?' enquired Shaun, his confusion mounting with every moment.

'The sommelier.' The man looked at Shaun as if he were rather slow on the uptake. 'The wine waiter. Ready to do our wine tasting? *We* certainly are.'

'Ah,' Shaun replied, 'I think there must be some mista...'

'Now then, let's get down to business,' the man cut in, rubbing his big rough hands together expectantly. 'I'm Captain Radish; served with the Major in France, don't you know. This is Mr. and

Mrs. Snodgrass: Chairman of the Bridge Club and his wife, who is the membership secretary. That's Lord Higginbottom,' he indicated a heavily moustached man sitting on the opposite side of the table who seemed to be studying the carpet. 'Ha; he's fallen asleep already. Often happens. Not to worry. This lady is the Right Honourable Candida Chumley-Smythe whose horse won the Derby at Epsom last year. I expect you've heard of her.'

Shaun shook his head, but Captain Radish didn't seem to notice as he plunged on.

'All present and correct; let's crack on shall we?'

With that, the Major dumped his overcoat into Shaun's arms and took a seat at the head of the table. The Right Honourable Candida Chumley-Smythe flashed a smile at Shaun as she followed suit and draped her fur coat on top of the Major's.

'Charmed,' she murmured as she sat herself down in a wave of lily-of-the-valley perfume and chiffon.

Shaun wasn't at all sure what was going on, but he backed carefully out of the room, barely able to see over the top of the accumulated coats. He dropped them gratefully onto a chair in the kitchen and scratched his head. What were all these people doing at Grandad's house? Was he supposed to entertain them? Give them tea? What had that man been saying about wine? He reached to put the kettle on, as he did so often at Grandad's house, and then caught sight of the flyer he had been reading earlier.

Of course. This must be The Bridge Club — or some of it — and they were here for the wine tasting event; but they had come too soon. It was the wrong day! Grandad wasn't even here.

As he looked more closely at the invitation, Shaun saw that the '8' on the '18th' of the month hadn't been printed very well; it had printed more like a '3'. These people must have thought it said the 13th — they were five days too early. Total disaster! No wonder Grandad wasn't ready for them. He would be so cross with himself for not being there.

As I've already told you, Shaun loved his Grandad very much, and the thought of him being embarrassed because he'd let his friends down was unthinkable, even if it was all a big mistake. Shaun thought quickly and made a decision. He wasn't sure what any of the guests were expecting, but he would certainly try provide a memorable experience if he could. He was very keen to protect Grandad's reputation.

He popped his head around the dining-room door. 'I'll be with you in two ticks,' he announced, and ran up the stairs two at a time and into Grandad's room. He threw open the wardrobe, stripped off his ratty T-shirt and lobbed his baseball cap on the bed.

'Come on Shaun,' he told himself sternly, 'you can do this.'

So saying, he pulled on one of his Grandad's white shirts, ironed to within an inch of its life. It was too big of course, but he rolled up the sleeves and tucked the bottom into his shorts. Not ideal, but it would have to do. Scrabbling around, he found a spotted bow tie on elastic and hurriedly added it to the outfit, pushing the elastic underneath the starched colour, out of sight. He glanced in the mirror and was surprised to see a dishevelled looking person staring back at him. This wouldn't do.

Carefully, he took the lid off Grandad's gloopy hair gel and smeared it over his head, smoothing his hair down into an unaccustomed style. If only he had a moustache like the chap downstairs he would look older; but he didn't, so, giving his improved reflection a last look, Shaun hurried back downstairs to greet the guests again.

'Gooood after-noon,' he said attempting a rather poor French accent. 'My name is Pierre and I would like to welcome to you to our unique wine tasting experience.'

That wasn't a lie. It would certainly be a one-off, Shaun thought to himself.

'Lovely,' purred The Right Honourable Candida Chumley-Smythe.

'Rather!' enthused Captain Radish.

'Excellent,' said Mr. Snodgrass.

Mrs. Snodgrass, sitting opposite her husband, smiled and nodded while Lord Higginbottom, sitting next to her, woke up with a start.

'Good gracious, have we started?' he asked, and promptly went straight back to sleep.

Shaun was relieved, and amused, to find that none of the guests seemed to notice he was the same person

who'd taken their coats a few minutes before. He moved to the old-fashioned dresser where Grandad kept his wine glasses alongside the set of china he and Granny had had as a wedding present sixty

years ago or more. Some quick maths showed there were enough for each guest to have five.

'Monsieur,' Shaun began with the Captain, who seemed to think of himself as the most important person there. Getting into character, Shaun placed the glasses down with what he hoped was a professional flourish.

'Madam,' he moved on to The Right Honourable Candida Chumley-Smythe, and returned to the dresser for some more. Mr. and Mrs. Snodgrass and Lord Higginbottom were attended to as well, and soon everyone had their five wine glasses in front of them.

Shaun hurried back to the kitchen and took stock of the situation. Suddenly it dawned on him: how could he have forgotten? The wine cellar was locked. There was no wine to be tasted; not a drop! What on earth was he going to do? He didn't know anything about any of it, anyway. Panic was beginning to rise from somewhere in his tummy as he began to search for the cellar key. He looked on the window sill; in the kitchen drawers; on top of the fridge; underneath the egg-timer. He found three dead woodlice and a squashed fly, but no key.

'OK Shaun,' he told himself, 'take a breath and calm down. You can't use real wine. What can you use instead?'

Encouraged by his own steadier thoughts, he went to the fridge and looked eagerly inside. He would just have to produce five different flavoured drinks out of whatever he could find and hope Grandad's guests didn't notice. If he kept talking long enough, perhaps he could distract them from the contents of their glasses.

His eye fell on the guava juice he'd just had, and some lemonade. He'd start with that. Pulling an empty bottle out of the recycling bin – thank goodness Grandad hadn't emptied it recently – he washed it out under the tap and half-filled it with juice. The lemonade was poured on top until it fizzed up over the sides. Yanking open a drawer, Shaun found a freshly laundered tea towel which he draped over one arm before heading back to the guests.

He wasn't sure he would get away with this charade and his hands trembled a little as he poured a couple of centimetres of the liquid into each glass.

'Ladies and gentlemen,' he began, temporarily forgetting his accent, but adjusting quickly. 'Madams and messieurs,' which was about the extent of his French anyway, 'we begin with this particular wine…'

'Ah,' said Mrs. Snodgrass approvingly. 'A sparkling rosé. My favourite.'

'Oh yes; oui, a rosé madam,' Shaun quickly agreed. It was certainly the colour of pink roses, so if that was the official term he was happy to go along with that. The plan might actually work if he could only keep it up.

Mr. Snodgrass held his glass up to the light. 'What do you think dear? A strong colouring?' he asked his wife.

'Oh yes, more than the usual blush,' she agreed, examining the contents of her glass in the same way.

Shaun nodded as if he had just been about to say the same thing.

'Indeed; oui, oui.'

Captain Radish picked up his glass and sniffed it noisily.

'What do you think Harold?' enquired Mrs. Snodgrass. 'What are you getting on the nose?'

Shaun felt a giggle wriggle up into his mouth, but didn't dare let it out, so he disguised it as a high-pitched cough. What strange language these people used to talk about wine. The only thing he'd ever got on the nose was a severe bump followed by a nose bleed when he'd walked into

Grandad's patio doors thinking they were open when they weren't. Grandad had let him stick a transfer on them after that so he wouldn't make the same mistake again.

'Quite fruity,' declared the Captain with absolute certainty. The other drinkers nodded in agreement, except for Lord Higginbottom who had simply nodded off.

The Bridge Club who were still awake, all swirled the juice in their glasses and sniffed again. Shaun wondered if anyone would ever actually drink it and whether any of them would notice it was just guava juice and lemonade after all.

'I'm getting some jasmine,' Mrs Snodgrass announced.

'Really?' Her husband sniffed his own glass again. 'Not picking that up Maud. Interesting.'

The Right Honourable Candida Chumley-Smythe allowed her delicate nose to hover over the top of her pink drink, but sniffed so mildly she barley appeared to breathe in at all.

'Perhaps you might all like to try it now?' suggested Shaun, his French accent faltering somewhat. The tension was killing him; he needed to know whether his trick was working or not.

A ripple of 'Absolutely's went around the room. Glasses were tilted as sips were taken.

Shaun held his breath; this was the moment of truth.

'Mmmm,' murmured the ladies.

'Not bad at all,' said Mr. Snodgrass.

Captain Radish wrinkled his nose, and the tasters leaned forward a little to hear his opinion which seemed to matter to them the most.

'You know, this reminds me of something...'

'Ah,' Shaun jumped in, desperately thinking of a suitable reply that would distract them all from the truth. ' Er… holidays perhaps? A refreshing drink for a hot afternoon on the beach maybe..?'

'Oh yes,' whispered The Right Honourable Candida Chumley-Smythe as she took another sip. 'Perfectly marvellous!'

Shaun realised he was still holding his breath, and let it out in a rush.

The Right Honourable lady continued in her lilting voice: 'Imagine drinking this on one's yacht at Cannes!' She gave a little gasp of excitement. 'It would be perfect with oysters. What is it?' She turned her violet eyes towards Shaun.

'Erm, well…' Shaun racked his brains. He hadn't expected this question and now, with mounting horror realised he would have to make up names for every concoction he served. 'It's a new blend,' he said quite truthfully.

'Oh yes,' murmured The Right Honourable Candida Chumley-Smythe, 'very young, very vibrant.'

Was she talking about him or the guava and lemonade mix? Shaun wasn't sure.

'Yes…er…oui,' he burbled. 'Madam is so right. It is made from the freshest fruit…' Shaun suddenly remembered the picture of a colourful festival on the packet of juice and, with a shot of inspiration, continued, 'from India.'

'Ah!' exclaimed Captain Radish bringing his hand down on the table with a crash which woke Lord Higginbottom on his left. 'Should have guessed that. Probably Rajasthan. Very big on carnivals there. It's not usually my scene and to tell the truth, I'm not really a sparkling wine man, but it makes sense that this one carries that kind of keynote.'

'Oui, oui,' Shaun hurriedly agreed. 'Carnival wine; festival vibe. Monsieur is correct; absolutely. It is a party wine for celebration.'

'Super,' declared Mr. Snodgrass. 'Higginbottom! What do you think?'

His neighbour, who had woken so abruptly, spotted the full glass in front of him and swallowed the contents in one swift gulp. He smacked his sticky lips together and smiled.

'Tastes like candy floss,' he proclaimed. 'Reminds me of Brighton 1962, on the pier. Lovely girl; lived in Clapham I believe.'

Mrs. Snodgrass raised her eyebrows.

'Perhaps we should move on,' suggested her husband.

Shaun took the hint and hurried next door to mix another 'wine', mightily relieved that he had got this far successfully.

Spotting the wine magazine on the counter top, he opened it eagerly with one hand while pouring the surplus guava-lemonade down the sink. The contents page listed white wines and then red. Following the pattern Shaun decided he would somehow have to make two whites and two reds if he was to pull off this fake tasting.

He opened the larder door and scanned the shelves. What was there that could pass for white wine and not be recognised? White vinegar would be detected immediately; cooking oil would be too greasy; sugar dissolved in water? Shaun wasn't sure about that. Back to the fridge. No; milk was too solid a colour; salad dressing had herbs floating in it and there was no apple juice. Back to the larder again. Shaun started to feel desperate. He shifted tins and packets, looking for something that would do. Finally his eyes fell on two bottles of squash: orange and blackcurrant. Could he do something with those? He grabbed the orange and went back to *Viticulture Today* on the counter.

The first white wines were described as buttery, with hints of honey and butterscotch. There had been honey in the cupboard, which Shaun quickly found again. Rinsing another bottle from recycling, he put the tiniest bit of concentrated squash in it, filling it three quarters full with water so it was pale and weak. A quick squirt of honey and then, holding a cloth over the open top he shook it as hard as he could. Picking up a mug from the draining board, he poured a teensy bit in the bottom and, eyeing it suspiciously, sipped it cautiously.

It wasn't awful; but it wasn't great either. The honey definitely helped. Scanning the shelves again, he saw the vintage tin Granny had used for her cake-making bits and bobs. The lid was stiff but he managed to prise it off just as he heard the raised voices next door wondering where the next wine was. Shaun found what he wanted, undid the lid and added a few drops before shaking the wine bottle again, taking care to cover the open top.

'Pardon, pardon,' he laughed artificially as he returned to the dining room.

'Problem?' asked Captain Radish turning a searching stare on the pretend sommelier.

'Non, non.'

Shaun put his thumb and first finger apart a short distance then shrugged and waved his arms dismissively. He didn't know any other French words and hoped this would be enough to avoid further questions. Fortunately, it was; for now, at least.

'Ah,' said Mrs. Snodgrass appreciatively, 'a white.'

'Oui,' agreed Shaun, 'Madame is correct. A wine with another unique flavour, I'm sure you will all agree…'

Shaun poured a small amount of the new mixture into everyone's glass and took a step back. Once again, the tasters lifted their glasses to examine the colour of the wine. Even Lord Higginbottom gave it a cursory glance before holding it under his nose.

'Oh, humph; oh,' he grunted in a non-committal kind of way.

'What d'ya think Higgy?' asked his neighbour at the head of the table. 'Pretty strong, eh?'

'Hrumph.'

The Lord's moustache wiggled energetically as his large red nose wrinkled unattractively before taking a massive sniff of the new drink.

'Good gracious!' exclaimed Mrs. Snodgrass. 'How unusual. One doesn't usually get such a strong nose on a chardonnay. It is a chardonnay I assume?' She turned her head quizzically towards Shaun who nodded vigorously; he didn't want the discussions to take him into even deeper unknown territory.

'Oui, yes. Madam knows her wines.'

Shaun, of course did not have a clue but it seemed that flattering the guests was a good idea. He looked round the table, wondering how much he could steer the reactions of The Bridge Club.

'One is getting on the nose perhaps… something…?' he suggested, repeating what had been said previously.

'Madagascan vanilla,' breathed The Right Honourable Candida Chumley-Smythe, clearly carried away on a breeze of fantasy.

'Spot on Candy,' affirmed Mr. Snodgrass, using a shortening of her name which Shaun thought rather overly-friendly. His wife frowned opposite him, while keeping her nose firmly over her own glass.

Shaun was delighted; he had added some of Granny's vanilla essence as the final ingredient, but was worried it was too much.

'The vanilla, you have found!' He deliberately switched his words into a different order to sound less English. 'Congratulations. You like it, I think?'

'I do,' she said solemnly, 'and now I am going to taste it.'

There was a dramatic pause. Everyone in the room stopped to watch her lift the glass to her exquisite lips, her ringed and manicured hands elegant in the afternoon light. She seemed to flinch slightly and everyone drew in their breath sharply wondering what she was tasting. Shaun could see that she hadn't actually swallowed the wine, and found himself sweating nervously; imagining that this was the moment his plan would shatter into a thousand fragments.

The titled lady exhaled a small sigh, and lifted her glass towards the other tasters.

'Enjoy!' She smiled at them as she took another sip and everyone hurriedly picked up their own glass and made a 'Cheers' motion towards the middle of the table before tasting for themselves.

'Oh yes,' sighed Mrs. Snodgrass, 'the vanilla tone is coming through nicely.'

'I'm getting honey too,' chipped in Captain Radish.

'Honey?' asked Lord Higginbottom who had begun to drift off again. 'I love honey.'

He promptly swallowed his entire tasting portion in one go again, and closed his eyes blissfully.

'Wondering about the soil for this particular wine, Pierre.' Mr. Snodgrass looked hopefully at Shaun, who shifted his weight uncomfortably and pretended he was thinking about it. What in the world was the man talking about?

'I imagine it's limestone-based,' his wife interrupted.

Shaun was grateful for her intervention. It made sense that different vines flourished on different types of soil, just the same as other plants; but he didn't know anything about that either. Agreeing seemed a good option.

'Madam is correct again; oui, of course. Limestone for honey chardonnay.'

He wondered how much he could make up about this wine but, fortunately, the Bridge Club seemed happy to weave their own stories.

Feeling more confident, Shaun returned to the kitchen for another quick recipe. His choices were limited but he decided to make the orange squash a tiny bit stronger this time. The magazine talked about 'citrus notes, freshly cut grass and green peppers'. Working quickly with another bottle, he used less water with the concentrated liquid and added a squeeze of fresh lemon from the fridge. He didn't think putting grass in the mixture was a good idea, but he did add a small slice of green pepper he found in the salad drawer at the bottom of the fridge, shook the bottle vigorously – being careful to cover the top, of course – and hoped the flavour would penetrate the overall orange-ness.

The chatter in the dining room was getting louder and the laughter more frequent, though Shaun noticed on his return that Lord Higginbottom's head was now almost resting on the table as he snoozed. He poured a small amount into everyone's third glass and waited to see what would happen.

Once again, and to Shaun's enormous relief, The Bridge Club seemed happy to come to their own conclusions.

'Fascinating colour,' said Captain Radish, holding his glass up to the light.

'Captivating bouquet,' observed Mrs. Snodgrass.

'Refreshing on the palate,' declared Mr. Snodgrass.

'Enthralling,' agreed 'Candy', sipping her 'wine' with a far away look in her eyes.

'Zzzzzzzz,' snored Lord Higginbottom.

Shaun could barely believe his luck. He hugged himself in delight. How were they not noticing this was basically ordinary orange squash?

His confidence was so boosted that he began to lift phrases he remembered from the magazine. He started to talk about *notes of green pepper* and, encouraged by his audience's rapt attention, began exaggerating wildly. 'Hints of cabbage... whispers of spring... essence of seaweed... echoes of childhood.'

'Not quite getting that Pierre,' frowned Captain Radish, 'perhaps you could pour me a little more?'

Shaun hastily obliged and bit his lip before he got too carried away. He needed to be careful and not mess this up for Grandad now he'd got this far.

Around the table there was a certain amount of muttering. Their initial enthusiasm appeared to be waning, although nothing seemed to disturb the quiet contentment of The Right Honourable Candida Chumley-Smythe.

Perhaps it was time to go and mix a 'red wine' before things unravelled.

Back in the kitchen, Shaun picked up the blackcurrant squash. This would have to be the base of his last two 'wines'. A quick look back at *Viticulture Today* told him that these wines were fruity, often tasting of berries and sometimes with flavours of spice, smoke, leather or earthiness. Gross! Why would anyone enjoy the taste of mud? Shaun couldn't understand it. Pushing that thought aside for the time being, he tried to concentrate again. How in the world was he going to pull this off?

Two more bottles were retrieved from the recycling bin and rinsed out. Shaun poured a couple of centimetres of blackcurrant into one and twice as much into the other. Scanning the larder for inspiration he found a dusty tin of plums. He scrabbled in the drawer for a tin opener and managed to prise the lid off, narrowly avoiding slicing his thumb open. Spooning the plums out into a bowl, he poured the remaining juice into the first bottle, filled the rest with water and went through the shaking routine. That would count for one of the 'wines'.

Remembering there had been some beetroot next to the green peppers, Shaun rescued one. Slightly shrivelled, they were still a fantastic colour, though Shaun had always thought they tasted slightly muddy. Perhaps that was the same as 'earthy'? He had no idea, but he didn't think that adding actual mud from the garden was an idea worth pursuing. He sliced a piece off, squashed it in another bowl with the back of a fork and pushed it into the second bottle adding a sprinkle of cinnamon. Making up the volume with water, he covered the top again before shaking it gently to mix up all his ingredients.

Shaun took a last glance at the *Viticulture Today* to check the names of red wines. Some of them were unpronounceable, but he saw a couple he thought would do.

A moment later, he was back in the dining room.

Mr. Snodgrass had been pouring the contents of the last glass into a pot plant on the window sill just as Shaun came in, and he quickly sat down again looking slightly embarrassed.

'Not sure about that last one, Pierre,' he said.

Shaun noted that Captain Radish hadn't drunk all his either and Mrs. Snodgrass was sucking a peppermint to take the taste away. Perhaps the green pepper and been a mistake. His plan was

looking rather shaky right now; he'd have to work really hard to regain credibility.

'Pas de problem; no problem,' he answered, slipping clumsily into his semi-French accent again. 'We are coming now to our reds.' He held up the bottles for the guests. 'An unusual Merlot and, I think you will agree, a rather special Malbec.'

The wine tasters looked more enthusiastic again, as Shaun poured a little of each into their remaining two glasses.

'Perhaps you can compare them together,' he suggested, trying to move things along. Frankly, the sooner this was over, the better.

'Our first is a wonderful wine with plum on the nose and a hint of berries on the mouth.' Shaun was really getting into his stride with the descriptions now. *Viticulture Today* had been a real life-saver; thank goodness Grandad had left a copy to hand.

The familiar examining, swirling and sniffing was going around the table. Even Lord Higginbottom was awake again and taking part.

'Oh yes,' breathed Candy, 'this smells divine!'

There were sounds of agreement and greedily, everyone drank.

'You are tasting the flavour, I think?' Shaun/Pierre asked them all, hoping that they would like this strange mixture enough to believe it was real.

'Strong aftertaste; very good,' said the now attentive Lord appreciatively, pushing his glass forward hopefully. Shaun poured him a little more, and although no alcohol had been in any of the non-wine 'wines', the atmosphere was changing before his eyes. Everyone was laughing, joking and talking increasingly loudly. The 'reds' seem to have kicked off a party.

Shaun decided to take advantage of the moment and press on with his last wine so he could get this nightmare over with. He knew that he couldn't keep this up much longer.

'Now,' he said, 'you will be smelling the spices of the east in this glass. It will slide across your tongue with ease I think. You will tell me how you find it now please.'

The Right Honourable Candida Chumley-Smythe was obviously having a dreamy afternoon. She had sniffed, swirled and sipped and now sat back with her eyes closed in delight.

'Flying carpets,' she sighed.

Shaun felt rather alarmed. Was she tasting dusty carpet or imagining one?

'No, no,' Mrs. Snodgrass disagreed. 'This is Christmas in a glass. I must order some for the Bridge Club members party this year. It's perfect, Pierre. The Major will give me the details I'm sure.'

'Perfect,' agreed her husband.

Shaun swallowed nervously. How one earth would he be able to make a whole batch of this stuff without people realising it was plain old blackcurrant squash with a few extras thrown in? Where would he get so many bottles from… and labels…? He could feel a trickle of sweat rolling down his back from sheer stress now. How, for that matter, would he be able to face Grandad? Perhaps this hadn't been such a good idea. Suddenly, from teething on the brink of disaster, it was working far too well.

Lord Higginbottom scraped his chair backwards and rose unsteadily to his feet.

'I would like to propose a toast,' he announced; 'to wine, to memories, to our absent host and our fine sommelier.'

Shaun blushed as everyone rose to their feet and lifted their glasses, repeating the sentiment with gusto, laughter and applause.

And that is why no one had heard the front door open, or footsteps in the hall, or the crash of a skateboard.

Shaun himself was just taking an awkward bow, when Grandad walked into the room nursing a bruised shin and with a look of undisguised astonishment on his face.

'What in the blazes…?'

He stopped short on seeing a portion of The Bridge Club in his dining room, apparently being entertained by his grandson, who was parading around the room with two open wine bottles, a wonky bow tie, and dressed in a shirt that the Major recognised as his own.

For a moment Shaun froze, staring at Grandad, a mixture of acute discomfort and anxiety on his face, while Grandad opened his mouth to say something but couldn't.

'I can explain,' Shaun began.

'Can you?' Grandad asked sternly.

'Er, no… not really.' Shaun's jaunty exuberance left him like bubbles from a can of drink, and his Pierre pretence fizzled away in much the same way.

It was Captain Radish who stepped in.

'Major! Where've you been? We missed you. Capital wine tasting this afternoon.'

'Wine...?' Grandad's confused face spoke volumes, and he turned a hard stare on his grandson.

'Hiring a sommelier was a genius idea,' said Mr. Snodgrass helping himself to the remains of the pretend Malbec.

'I... I don't understand,' stammered Grandad. 'You're all coming next week. What's going on?'

So finally, the story was told and Shaun owned up to his non-wine wine-tasting drama. Grandad was so relieved that his collection hadn't been broken into, and so touched by his grandson's efforts to save him from embarrassment that he couldn't help but laugh. The guests were a little more subdued as they realised that they had spent an afternoon drinking an extremely odd collection of ordinary fruit squashes; beverages that the wine-makers of the world would have been outraged to know had been passed off as their own.

Nevertheless, The Right Honourable Candida Chumley-Smythe kissed Shaun on both cheeks before she floated out of the house, quite undaunted by the strange afternoon. Mrs. Snodgrass did not ask for the name of the supplier of the final wine, having decided that a fruit punch would do very well for the Bridge Club Christmas party. Mr. Snodgrass shuffled out without looking at Shaun; he was kicking himself for not realising that he had been taken in by the afternoon's activity and was feeling rather foolish. Lord Higginbottom hurried home for what he considered, a well-deserved nap. Captain Radish laughed loud and long, partly because he was also rather uncomfortable about the whole affair, and partly because his friend the Major ranked above him. The memory of their time together in France all those years ago meant that he would always support his commanding officer.

Once they had all sorted out which coat belonged to whom, and crunched their way down the drive again, Grandad turned towards Shaun.

'My boy, I'm proud of you,' he announced, expressing his admiration for Shaun's creativeness as they both cleaned up the kitchen and carefully washed and dried the precious glasses.

He guffawed all over again when he heard the whole story.

'I think you'll make a first class sommelier one day.'

Shaun blushed and thanked his lucky stars that he was not in trouble. It had been an extremely odd afternoon. He was in no hurry to repeat it, or anything like it.

'Thanks Grandad. I think I'll stick to skateboarding for now.'

Grandad was still laughing the next week when The Bridge Club returned in force for the real wine tasting on the 18th of the month, when he dazzled them with his expert knowledge and stories, as well as with some truly exquisite wines which were enjoyed by all. Especially by Lord Higginbottom who, surprisingly, stayed awake throughout and could be heard softly talking to himself: 'Brighton 1962. Extraordinary.'

Sovereign Secrets

Sovereign Secrets

You may already know the peculiar history of the fascinating kingdom of Slopingsideways.

This was the nation which was cut off from the rest of the world for an entire century – the consequence of some devastating floods. It had been a sleepy and relaxed place, where there was always time to lean on a gate and watch the sun set. However, that changed almost overnight when it was discovered, a hundred years later, that the water had receded. The kingdom joined up with the rest of the world again, and was subsequently inundated with so many gadgets and gizmos that everyone became rather overwhelmed and yet, mysteriously, still short of time.

The invention with the biggest impact had been the mobile phone, which proved to be such a distraction that, for a while, life pretty much ground to a halt from the palace to the pavement. Thanks to the unprecedented performance of the famous soprano opera singer, Dame Vera Wobblington at the first, post rejoining-the-rest-of-the-world Annual Arts Festival, a high note of such pitch was reached that it reverberated across the country causing all the brand new phone masts to collapse. After this, a thorough review had been undertaken, and common sense had mostly returned. Life in Slopingsideways began to, more or less, resemble life in neighbouring countries as the years of disconnection slipped away from memory.

This was all very well, except in the royal palace where things, unfortunately, were far from well.

The King pushed his half-eaten toast away and humphed loudly, causing the Queen to look up from her cornflakes.

'What's the matter, Arthur?' she enquired patiently.

'Oh, I don't know,' he grumbled, fiddling with his coffee cup and rattling the spoon around on the saucer; a habit she found extremely irritating.

Her Majesty wisely bit her lip in order to hold back a sharp comment and, instead, took a deep breath and lifted her own traditional cup of tea to her mouth.

'Can I help at all?' she offered, with admirable tact, before taking a ladylike sip.

'Oh, I don't know,' her husband repeated testily. 'I just don't know anything anymore.'

Clearly, this was not true; but his wife forbore to say anything that might be considered unhelpful, or fan the flames of his obvious discontent.

The King stabbed at the butter with undisguised vexation until it looked as though it had been stomped on by particularly athletic amateur folk dancers who didn't know their steps very well. Abandoning that activity with another sigh, he pushed his chair back so it balanced on two legs – something else that his wife found both irritating and dangerous (you may have been told off for this yourself from time to time), and threw his crumpled napkin onto the table scattering toast crumbs onto the floor.

The Queen put down her spoon and fixed a gaze on him which she hope communicated everything she wouldn't allow herself to say at that point.

'You know, Adelaide,' he sighed wearily, 'I think, perhaps, I'm just bored.'

'Bored?' The Queen's eyebrows disappeared under her new fringe. She was trying out a modern hairstyle as recommended by the royal hairdresser, but wasn't yet convinced that it was quite 'her'.

'Arthur, how can you be bored?' she continued. 'You're the King for heaven's sake. We've a whole country to rule; official visits to make; diplomatic visitors to host. Our diaries are packed to bursting.'

'I know, I know,' he blustered; 'but it's not the same is it?'

His wife looked at him with her head on one side, awaiting further explanation.

'The Prime Minister and government do most of the ruling these days and take responsibility for a lot of those things. I'm not sure how many more ribbons I want to go and cut, or speeches I want to listen to about things that don't interest me very much.'

There was a sharp intake of breath from the other end of the breakfast table.

'It's your job, Arthur. You know that.'

She could see her husband squirming.

'Yes, dear; yes I do. Duty and all that. But the thing is, now we have so much of our administration done by computer, and communication is so much faster, it's freed up a lot more time. Things have been streamlined so much, I don't feel as though I'm needed in the same way. I don't want to make any more models out of matchsticks, and the stamp collection is dull. The doctor won't let me try parachuting or white water rafting any more. I know you don't want me to go back to using my phone every day...'

That was absolutely true. The Queen had been driven almost to distraction by her husband's infatuation with the dragon-blasting game on his mobile phone. She had wasted hours sending people to look for him in unlikely places when he'd failed to appear at important meetings, because he was hiding away somewhere trying to boost his score.

What was also uncomfortably true was that, as her husband explained his dilemma, she had a terrible feeling that she was also beginning to feel rather bored. She no longer enjoyed some of her more energetic hobbies – last time she'd been horse riding, she'd been sore for a fortnight – she wanted to do something more creative. Every day had become too much like the previous ones. It was all very predictable and, yes; rather boring. Technology, and so-called progress, had changed everything. She was still a huge fan of leaning on gates and watching the sunset, but that still left an awful lot of hours in the day. It was very unsettling.

The King rocked his chair back onto the four legs for which it was designed, and stood up.

'I'm sorry, Adelaide. I don't want to burden you with this. I'm sure you have enough to think about yourself.'

He walked around the table and planted an affectionate kiss on her royal forehead.

'I'll work it out eventually, I'm sure.'

So saying, he left the room.

The Queen was left nursing what remained of her now soggy cereal; a barely recognisable inedible sludge at the bottom of the bowl. She too turned her thoughts to ways of relieving her own growing discontent with her life. She had always been a positive person; a problem solver and energetic achiever; but recently she'd found herself wishing life had never changed at all in Slopingsideways.

Perhaps, it had been boredom which had prompted her to try this new hairstyle. If it was, then it hadn't worked; she was finding herself at a loose end way too frequently and, as you know, there are only so many times you can rearrange the contents of your sock drawer.

She was still lost in thought, when the maid came in to clear the table.

'Sorry ma'am; I thought you'd both left,' she apologised.

'It's fine, Jemima. It is Jemima, isn't it?' the Queen double-checked. She prided herself on knowing the names of every one of her staff, but there had been some changes recently. What with one thing and another, she wasn't as sure of herself this morning.

'Yes ma'am,' Jemma bobbed a curtsey and wondered whether it was alright to put down her tray and start clearing the breakfast debris.

'Do carry on, Jemima. I'm so sorry; I should have left by now. I was thinking.'

Jemima guessed correctly that Her Majesty was not looking for a reply, so said nothing.

The Queen sighed – there had already been a great deal of sighing this morning – and tried to clear her thoughts.

'Are you ever bored, Jemima?' she asked.

Jemima found this both an unexpected and a difficult question. She hadn't been at the palace long and was only allowed in the breakfast room today because Audrey, who usually had this task, was off sick with a nasty chest infection. If she said, 'Yes,' she might be in trouble and consequently given loads more work to do. She wasn't sure she was going to get the approval of the housekeeper to stay beyond her six week trial period as it was. On the other hand, 'No,' wasn't a completely truthful answer.

Her Sovereign clearly had something on her mind, so she decided to fudge it.

'Not often, Ma'am.' It seemed the safest reply.

'And when you are…?' The Queen was definitely looking for more.

'Well, I sometimes read a book or watch a television programme. I once took a dance class which was quite fun.'

'That's interesting; tell me more.'

Jemima began to feel little under pressure.

'Umm… it was an evening class. I went with my friend. We'd been watching a dance series on television and fancied having a go. We signed up at the library or online or something, ma'am. It was for eight weeks and we saved up to pay for it out of our wages.'

'And were you any good?' The Queen was genuinely interested, but Jemima didn't want to tell her that she'd been rubbish, and had found herself moving as though she had two left feet and the grace of an arthritic rhinoceros.

Instead she said, 'My friend was very good.'

The Queen smiled, understanding completely and said, 'I imagine it was a lot of fun.'

'It was, ma'am,' Jemima agreed heartily.

'Marvellous,' concluded the Queen as she picked a limp cornflake from her lap and went to her study with the merest speck of an idea floating around her head.

Meanwhile, His Majesty had been trawling through the ideas on his computer. In a mixture of desperation and frustration, he had typed in the question, *what should I do if I'm bored?* A slew of answers came up. There was no shortage of ideas.

He began to make notes:

Learn to cook

Join a club

Take up a sport

Call a friend

Write a journal

Make a home movie

Sew a piece of clothing

Do a jigsaw

Learn a language

The lists were long and varied. He had expected to experience the sense of a bright neon sign flashing over one specific thing, guiding him. He didn't, and consequently, he was disappointed.

He was about to give up when his eye was caught by an advert scrolling along the bottom of the screen.

Don't let your talents go down the drain, it announced. *Train as a plumber with our professionals. Ring for details.*

He snorted with good humour.

'*Go down the drain…* very good. That's rather clever.' He chortled to himself for a while, appreciating the play on words.

'I wonder,' pondered His Majesty, and cautiously reached for the phone.

At that moment, his wife was also wondering whether there wasn't some new skill that she could learn too. Her mother had taught her how to knit, years ago. She was already a fairly good cook, though there weren't many opportunities to use that skill in a palace where chefs were on hand to rustle up anything from a boiled egg to a banquet at a moments notice. She had toyed with painting at one time. One of her watercolours was still hanging up at the back of her wardrobe where no one else could see it. With so many valuable works of art on the palace walls, she couldn't really have her own painting on display; but it was sometimes nice to glimpse it on the wall behind her formal dresses.

Oil paints, she recalled, had proved rather messy back then. They were extremely gloopy, and had left stubborn, ugly stains that had refused to come out of her clothes, despite some serious scrubbing. A combination of an unfortunate spillage and her mother's severe scolding had seen the end of that venture.

But...

A thought plopped into the royal head with the same sort of 'kersploosh' as a stone dropping into a pond. She didn't fancy Jemima's dance class, but perhaps she could step up the scale and type of her painting. The more she mused, the more the Queen liked the idea. The thought of doing something fresh, and learning a new skill perked her up. Perhaps she should suggest it to Arthur. On second thoughts, she didn't want him to know that she'd also been feeling bored. He might think she was letting the side down.

She opened the laptop which she had leaned to use when technology flooded into Slopingsideways, and began to type.

It was a fortnight later, when Her Majesty found a set of overalls bundled up in the shed, that she began to get into her stride. She'd been searching for something to wear for the painting and decorating evening class she'd signed up for; these were perfect. Sneaking them back to her room, she locked the door and struggled out of the dress she'd been zipped into that morning. As you know, clothes with zips in the back are particularly tricky to zip and unzip by yourself. Not surprisingly, there was the unmistakable sound of fabric ripping; but, by persistent wriggling, she eventually escaped. The overalls wouldn't have fitted over the top of the dress, but she found an old T-shirt at the back of one her drawers from a royal team-building exercise, which worked a treat underneath. No one would be able to see the slogan: *Royalty rocks* (the weekend had involved some nerve-wracking climbing challenges). She needed to be unrecognisable at her class; perhaps the fringe would help, especially if accessorised with a large hat, oversized earrings and some sunglasses.

Her husband however, was dismayed to discover that the overalls he thought he'd hidden so carefully were now, inexplicably, gone. He'd only popped them into the shed while he slipped below stairs to look for some spare boots in his size which could be worn at his new evening class. He was delighted to discover some old galoshes (which are like waterproof gardening shoes); they seemed highly suitable, and he sneaked out again before the butler, who was busy preparing a tea tray for elevenses, saw him.

He too, had no wish to be recognised by anyone inside or outside the palace. It would be a challenge to attend the intense weeks of training without anyone finding out, but he was invigorated by the prospect of banishing boredom and embracing a new challenge. Since his face – and his wife's come to that – was on all the coins, bank notes and stamps currently in use, it would be tough to stay anonymous.

Now he would have to order the overalls online. If he had them sent under a different name his secret would still be safe. Adelaide always asked questions about parcels.

It was a Wednesday evening, shortly afterwards, when the Queen of Slopingsideways swept along the South Gallery towards the stairs, with a curiously bulging bag under her arm. Furtively dodging through the door to the backstairs, she almost collided with a heavily bearded man in a scruffy flat cap. She had no idea who he was – probably a visiting electrician (the landing light had been flickering a lot recently) – but had no time to make conversation. He let her go through before him, with a polite nod, and then followed her down the steps without speaking. Quietly closing the door to the room where the staff were gathered to review the day, she opened the outside door as though it might explode at any moment, skipped lightly through the puddles, and ran into an outside store room.

The hairy man registered puzzlement before also emerging into the damp evening, grabbing a bicycle he had prudently left leaning against the garden wall, and cycling off speedily, down the drive. Had he waited five more minutes, he would have noticed a lady of about the same age as himself emerging from an outbuilding, dressed in an odd collection of garments including an enormous purple sun hat. Of these, the sunglasses looked especially out of place considering both the time of day and the weather.

Thursday breakfast was a much jollier affair than either royal individual had experienced for some time. Both had attended their first class – a lucky

coincidence that they fell on the same day – and both had managed to return without being missed, while still keeping the other completely in the dark. The Queen had tiptoed past her husband's room so as not to wake him only a few minutes before the King had returned and taken his shoes off to avoid treading on squeaky floorboards, as he crept past his wife's room. (Royalty have long kept separate rooms. It avoids the problem of loud snoring, or the tricky consequences of one enjoying late nights while the other rises early for all the royal duties that are required of them.)

'You seem chipper this morning, Arthur,' observed her Majesty, feeling very positive herself.

'Glorious day, Adelaide,' her husband observed, helping himself to two pieces of toast and an extra crispy piece of bacon. He smiled as he crunched it happily.

'All alright?' she asked, not wanting to give herself away with any news of her own.

'Capital, my dear. All good at my end of the table. You?'

'Also good; thank you for asking.'

They smiled at one another with genuine pleasure and then smiled again to themselves, protecting their secrets, and tucking in to what they had always been told was the most important meal of the day.

Things in the palace grew busier as preparations for the Slopingsideways Annual Arts Festival began to be discussed. It was only six months away, which is a long time when you're waiting for your birthday, but no time at all if you have to organise a national event. Thanks to the new technology, neither royal was required to trawl through piles of paperwork or give handwritten permission for things anymore. This provided more time to practise their skills in private and extend their understanding by reading online articles.

By the time the next Wednesday came around, neither could hide their excitement.

'You feeling quite well?' the King asked his wife over lunch.

She was humming while pushing a piece of salmon round her plate and chasing the accompanying salad with a well-practised fork.

'Yes, thank you, darling,' she replied breezily.

He gave a little snort. 'It's just that you seem rather distracted.'

'Do I?' she asked innocently. 'I can't think why. I'm just enjoying this delicious luncheon.'

She avoided his searching look as she speared a large radish. It made a satisfying crunch in her mouth and, after swallowing she looked up.

'I was actually wondering whether you were suffering from something.'

'Who me?' The King opened his eyes wide and hoped she wouldn't try to guess anything.

His wife had always been good at guessing what birthday present he had bought for her, or where he'd hidden a stash of chocolate biscuits. He wanted to keep his plumbing hush-hush for as long as possible.

'No, no, my dear. You're mistaken. Fit as a fiddle. Healthy as a horse. Well as a wallaby. Strong as a squid.' He snapped his mouth closed, concerned he was babbling. *Strong as a squid* – where had that come from?

'You're babbling, Arthur,' his wife frowned. He was definitely hiding something.

'Oh good; lemon meringue pie!'

The King changed the subject swiftly, and hurried off to check his equipment for class, taking his dessert with him.

It was just after the evening news when he hurried along the upstairs corridor, checking a number of specialist new tools in his (also new) canvas bag, when he caught a glimpse of someone disappearing downstairs in front of him. Why would any member of the staff be wearing a large purple hat? Unless the housekeeper had changed the in-house uniforms recently, it was odd to say the least. Since he was running little late, he dismissed the thought and quietly navigated the rest of the route. He had no wish to alert his wife to his new nocturnal outings.

The Queen was already well on the way to her own evening class, eager not to be late, and just as eager to keep up her disguise. She'd got away with it last week, and only hoped she could keep up the pretence. Fortunately she hadn't been required to say very much except her name, which she whispered to the tutor: 'Ada.' Her little brother had always called her that; Adelaide had been too difficult for a toddler to pronounce.

Over the next few weeks, while her husband was learning about drains, installing pipes, using power tools and trouble-shooting, she was having a marvellous time, drinking in information about gloss, matte, semi-gloss and enamel paints. She mastered brush-cleaning and roller care; learnt the properties of turpentine and methylated spirits; the importance of preparation: sanding, sugar soaping, and filling holes with a putty knife. She understood the importance of beginning with the ceiling when you are decorating, so that the paint doesn't drip on walls you've already painted. She started using terms like *cutting in*, and saw the sense in decorating the walls nearest the windows first, in any room, so you don't block the light as you work.

She was loving the opportunity to wield such a large paintbrush, splurging fabulous colours over large areas, or rolling it on in long, even strokes. Her talent on canvas definitely transferred to interior decorating, and there was no chance of being scolded by her mother any more. She had a good eye for combining different shades of colour which came with such fascinating, abstract labels. There were too many greens to count: *Lime Lush, Forest Fern, Coriander Carnival, Summer Grass, Apple Melody,*

Cucumber Fizz, Jungle Echo, Island Dream, Essence of Mint, Artichoke Medley... What a wonderful job somebody somewhere had, making up these exotic sounding names. Fortunately, there were lots of artificial walls at the evening class too, so every week she could practise her technique and revel in the wonderful spectrum of paints. She was soon getting the hang of plastering and considered taking a course in advanced wallpapering, to learn how to fit it smoothly around awkward plugs and sockets.

Her husband was having just as much fun on the other side of town, wrestling with washers and wrenches. Getting his hands dirty was an exhilarating experience for him, after so many years of watching other people do those sorts of dirty jobs. He discovered that it hadn't been half as much fun overseeing someone else as it was to roll up his own sleeves and dive into the messy jobs himself. He frequently found himself up to his elbows in muck, and was loving every minute.

He discovered the thrill of welding two pieces of metal pipe together, then checking it didn't leak when he ran water through it. Soon he was understanding how to prevent back flow – a term he had never come across before. The week they got to use a plunger to unblock a loo was a highlight; he whistled all the way home on his bicycle that night. (Strictly speaking, it was the gardener's bike, but that's another story). The Lord Chamberlain and head of security would have been horrified, and the Prime Minister may well have passed out completely had he known. Fortunately, they were blissfully unaware of any of this.

And still, both king and queen managed to keep their secret safe from one another for weeks and weeks.

There was a moment of near disaster at afternoon tea one day, when His Majesty asked her what the blue splodge was by her left ear. She pretended it was a bruise and hurriedly rearranged her hair to hide it.

Similarly, Her Majesty wondered why there was a strange looking tool on the sideboard at breakfast one morning. On enquiry, her husband quickly intervened and passed it to an under butler with a comment that it probably belonged in the shed, and must have been forgotten by some workman or other. She frowned – it seemed unlikely – but no more was said about it, and they moved on to other topics.

'Are we on schedule for the Arts Festival?' asked His Majesty, keen to change the subject. He didn't want to give his wife anymore time to think about his mistake with what was actually a drain cleaning implement. It had fallen out of his bag the previous night when he'd been rummaging for snacks after a particularly gruelling plumbing assignment at the evening class.

'As far as I know,' she said. 'I believe Dame Vera has been working on an entirely new selection of vocal pieces. The musical director did mention that there might be a guest appearance by a string quartet from somewhere or other. Was it Carletia, perhaps?'

'Splendid. That should attract some new audience members. I rather hope they don't repeat the marching bagpipers they flew in last year.' He shuddered at the memory.

The musical director, Harley Stave, had taken over the festival for the first time the previous year, after Sir Edmund Formby had retired. He had made the rookie error of trying to change too much too soon, and the bagpipes had not been a hit with anyone. Music critics likened their sound to that of a poorly cat expressing deep pain while a siren wailed in the background. It was not an experience that any one wanted repeated, least of all Mr. Stave who had been highly embarrassed and heavily criticised in newspaper reviews throughout Slopingsideways and beyond. Mr. Stave was, in fact, very well aware that he had misstepped, and even now was double checking that every performer was well rehearsed, up to scratch and melodic.

The theatre director, Irvin Garrick, who was in charge of everything except the musical programme itself, was having different challenges. He had been kept awake for several nights in a row, racked with anxiety about the state of the theatre structure.

The concert – always the grand final of the Annual Arts Festival – was to take place, as usual, in the Theatre Royal. This was a historic performance space which had been used for the past 200 years. The plush, red velvet seats had been reupholstered the year Dame Vera's performance had crashed the phone masts, so they were still in mint condition. The stage itself had some rather faded floorboards, but a bit of polish and a lot of elbow grease usually sorted that out.

There remained, however, the usual problem of their not being enough toilets, especially for the ladies, who were always forced to queue during the interval. The men managed pretty well and could be in and out of the facilities with time to spare. They could pay for three cornets, a packet of sweets and two different flavours of ice lolly while the poor ladies were still hopping from foot to foot, wondering if they'd make it back to their seats before the second half began.

Irvin Garrick was all too aware that new, modern, ladies toilets were a priority. He was also conscious that the process of applying for planning permission for old buildings can take years, and is a total nightmare. Town councils usually refuse in case somebody is upset that their great-uncle-twice-removed once had his photograph taken there with someone famous, or something similar. I think that is why this problem has gone on for so many years. Such a project would incur massive expense which would make a lot of people very angry very fast and, frankly, no one at the council wanted the hassle.

This did not make Irvin Garrick's life any easier. He made do with having a carpenter replace a few floorboards on the stage. This was just as well, since it turned out that this was a far bigger job than he'd imagined. Most of the boards were disintegrating, having been destroyed by woodworm. It would take a further six weeks for a crew of carpenters to complete the task. Mr. Garrick shuddered at the thought of having his name included in any newspaper review which reported that the great Dame Vera Wobblington had fallen through the floorboards mid-performance. It might very well have happened. The thought brought him out in a cold sweat. Thank goodness it had been discovered in time to make the necessary repairs. The poor man resorted to having two headache tablets and a long lie down before he could summon the energy to do anything else.

Other preparations, it seemed, were all under control. In the palace, as across the land, everyone in Slopingsideways began to look forward to the week-long festival, and wondered what might be included in the Grand Finale.

The Royal couple had now completed two terms of their evening classes. Both had a new spring in their step and twinkle in their eye. Each was unaware of how close they had so often come to discovering one another's secret. Several times they had passed on the stairs, or caught a glimpse of the other disappearing down the drive, or slipping into their room on their return. It was extraordinary that they hadn't blurted anything out, or left tell-tale equipment anywhere (apart from the unfortunate drain snake tool which had been accidentally left on the sideboard), and fairly miraculous that no member of staff had been alerted to what had been going on.

Both of them were now looking forward to classes resuming after the festival. They were no longer novices; each had shown great aptitude in their new skills and was progressing fast. They were currently wondering whether it might be time to share their new interest with their spouse.

The Queen was pondering this very thing on the morning of the concert dress rehearsal. It had been a wonderful week celebrating all things arty: acting, pottery, embroidery, ballet, rap music, mime, brass bands, weaving, sketching, collage, sewing, street dance, painting (not the kind she had been learning), crocheting, script-writing, sculpting, cinema; and more exhibitions, demonstrations and workshops than any one person could possibly have attended in the course of a single week. There was just one day to go before the Grand Finale concert.

The King arrived in the breakfast room at the same time as some fresh poached eggs, and rubbed his hands together in anticipation.

'Perfect start to the day,' he declared, helping himself to four. 'Nearly there, now. Looking forward to tomorrow, Adelaide?'

The Queen agreed that she was doing just that, and shifted in her chair, willing herself to share the secret she'd been carrying around for the last six months.

Not usually a woman who was lost for words, she found that she didn't know where to begin. Consequently, she decided she would wait until lunch time and try again then.

Lunchtime came and went. By the time afternoon tea was served on the terrace, she had got herself into such a state that she had to eat three scones and a tea cake before she felt able to say anything at all. The King had also been wondering how he could broach the subject of his evening plumbing escapades, and found he was struggling for a natural conversation. He went over some sentences in his head, and even practiced in front of the mirror a few times, but when he sat down with his wife, he came over all hot and bothered. The whole speech felt terribly forced, and he thought better of it.

Their flusterment (a word you won't find in the dictionary but which expresses their Majesties present state more accurately than most you will find there), was interrupted when the Lord Chamberlain arrived looking even more hot and bothered than they were, having just run up several flights of stairs and down again looking for the royal couple in umpteen rooms, all of which were empty (of people – not furniture; the palace was absolutely chock full of historic pieces). He was breathing heavily and looked unpleasantly sweaty; he was also clutching a hastily scribbled letter from Irvin Garrick.

'Majesties,' he panted. 'So sorry to disturb you. Emergency... at the theatre... excuse me.' The poor man was doubled over, desperately trying to get his breath back.

'Good heavens!' said His Majesty. Putting his knife down, he got up and took the note out of the Lord Chamberlain's clammy hand.

He scanned it quickly, muttered something under his breath, and left the room hurriedly.

His wife frowned; such bad manners were quite out of character.

Copying her husband's action, she left her place and picked up the note which had been dropped so hastily on the tablecloth.

'Good gracious!' said Her Majesty, abandoning her tea cake and racing up the stairs as fast as her dress allowed.

The remaining servants looked aghast at one another. What they had just witnessed had never happened before. The under butler, who was a little bolder, reached for the note himself.

Emergency! Blocked toilets have flooded the theatre.
Ceilings collapsed. Total disaster.
Alternative venue required immediately.
Please advise.

The young man's eyes widened considerably; this was devastating news. Where on earth would the Annual Festival closing concert be held now? Not only that, but since every worker in the country had a week off work during the festival to enjoy everything it had to offer, there wouldn't be any workers available to help. Sweeping the remnants of the rejected afternoon tea onto a silver tray, he popped a small macaroon in his mouth – something that was strictly forbidden – and thanked his lucky stars it wasn't his responsibility.

Upstairs, there was a flurry of activity in both the King and the Queen's apartments.

His Majesty grabbed his canvas bag full of tools and threw himself into his overalls before rushing pell-mell down the backstairs, barrelling through the outside door and grabbing the bicycle he'd been using for weeks from a rather surprised gardener, before pedalling to the theatre like a dervish.

Her Majesty also battled her way into her paint-splattered overalls, picked up her box of brushes, rollers and rags, and fled the palace grounds with her hair tied up in an old scarf.

Not surprisingly, her husband arrived first. Irvin Garrick was astounded to find himself face to face with the king, in the foyer. He didn't know whether to bow or make a hasty retreat to smarten up. He had been paddling his way around the theatre all afternoon without any shoes and with his trousers rolled up above the knee, assessing the considerable damage. His phone battery had died, which was why he'd sent a note to the palace (and as you know, water and electricity must absolutely never mix). As overseers of the festival, he didn't think he could hide this calamity from them.

His Majesty was not bothered about any of that today.

'Have you turned the water and electricity off?' he asked immediately, as so many plumbers do.

Irvin Garrick nodded.

'Well that's a good start,' His Majesty said. 'Get some people to swoosh all this water out of the building and show me where the problem is.'

The men were soon splashing their way past the ticket office, and heading for the ladies toilets in the upper circle.

Five minutes later, the Queen arrived, went through the double doors towards the stage, and took in the situation with an expert glance. It was a mess; that much was certain.

'Where is Mr. Garrick?' she asked a man with a mop. 'I need to see him immediately.'

The man gawped at her, unsure if his eyes were playing tricks on him.

'Aren't you...? You know, you really remind me of the...'

'Yes, yes,' Her Majesty replied, before he had time to complete his sentence. 'Yes, I am the Queen, thank you; but right now we need to move fast or the reputation of the Slopingsideways festival will be ruined. Get cracking now, my good man.'

The man – good or otherwise – gave an awkward bow and scuttled off, dripping as he went.

Mr. Garrick, when he appeared, was all apologies as he began to explain, bow and ask questions all at the same time.

'We've no time for that, Mr. Garrick,' his Sovereign admonished, 'there's a great deal to do here and obviously everyone else is on holiday except us and the festival volunteers. I don't suppose you've found a plumber? If so, I need to speak with him.'

The baffled theatre director escorted the Queen up the stairs to the offending toilets where she was flabbergasted to come face to face with her husband, who was replacing a cistern with impressive rapidity and a screwdriver.

'Arthur! What in the world are you doing here?'

The King looked up on hearing the familiar voice and was as startled as she was, not only on seeing her, but by her transformation. Never in his life had he seen his wife wearing such a combination of garments. He would have laughed had she not looked so very capable.

Of course, you can guess exactly what happened next, as the six months of sovereign secrets were finally explained. Mr. Garrick became increasingly confused as the royals giggled about false beards, chuckled over overalls, and finally descended into screams of laughter at the number of times they had seen each other without realising it.

Finally wiping the tears from their eyes, they congratulated one another on their resourcefulness and achievements. Once they had kissed one another on the cheek in congratulation, they got down to focusing on the current problem.

'It's a good job we did take those classes,' observed His Majesty. 'These toilets need to be replaced; they're outdated and the antique plumbing has deteriorated almost beyond repair. No one else is available to fix any of this, but I think I've got away with it this time. It needs to be sorted for tomorrow unless we cancel.'

'Oh, Arthur, we mustn't let that happen. Have you found the problem, do you think?'

Her husband waved a wrench at her as though it were a Slopingsideways flag during a parade.

'I have indeed. All sorted up here now. I think we covered this problem in week fifteen. How's it looking downstairs?'

'Horribly soggy,' the Queen replied. 'It's a shambles. Even once we've bailed out all the water, it will take months to dry out properly. We need some heaters to get started on the job. There's some damage to the stage wall, but I can paint that this afternoon once we've located a ladder. We can disguise it all and make it work – we've had quite a lot of practice at that, lately,' she grinned at her husband.

'Splendid,' he replied. 'In that case, I'm sure we don't need to find another venue.'

Irvin Garrick was instantly reassured, and scampered off immediately to begin drying out the auditorium. He was feeling enormously grateful that anyone had turned up to help, if somewhat staggered that it was the royals themselves. He had been hoping for a couple of kitchen staff at best, plus whoever else they could rope into joining them. That the show might really go on was a massive relief.

'The ceiling is another matter,' the Queen announced. 'I can't replaster it until it has dried out. The whole thing will need to come down now. However, I think we can make it safe enough for tomorrow if we can tie a strong canopy under it. That will catch any bits that are still loose. We can't have our Slopingsideways performers bashed on the head by falling debris.'

The rest of the day was filled with wringing out towels, squeezing water from carpets, positioning heaters, finding ladders, and collecting a huge piece of canvas from the Guild of Tent and Sailmakers. They were on holiday too but, fortunately, the Chair of the Guild was Jemima's uncle. Once his favourite niece had explained the dilemma, he was only too happy to help. Anything to make sure the national festival finished with the appropriate flourish.

The following evening, theatre-goers were buzzing with anticipation as they arrived for the much-anticipated concert. They were a little surprised to each be given a pair of shower caps to wear over their smart shoes (donated by the Slopingsideways Hospitality and Tourism Union). The carpet was still slightly squishy and Mr. Garrick didn't want anyone slipping over and suing the theatre, or demanding compensation for ruined footwear.

There was a lingering smell of drying paint in the air, but nobody was bothered that the performers all wore galoshes, and a variety of crash helmets. Nor were they aware that the ever-fabulous Dame Vera Wobblington had managed to transform a hard hat (health and safety regulations exist in Slopingsideways too, you know,) into a highly acclaimed statement piece of designer headgear, thanks to the addition of some beads, sequins, a variety of enormous feathers collected from the palace gardens (where peacocks shed them regularly), and a large purple sunhat donated by a certain well-wisher, and which fitted snugly over the top of it. This breath-taking accessory was admired by multiple reviewers, who devoted several column inches to it and influenced a significant number of theatre goers, who later tried to recreate it for themselves at home.

With surprisingly little flusterment, the King and Queen of Slopingsideways took their places in the royal box as the national anthem was played, before waving benevolently to the audience below, and admiring the newly painted back wall of the stage. Irvin Garrick had found several tins of *Sonata in D*, moonlight-blue paint underneath the stage, which had proved eminently suitable for redecorating. Her Majesty had enjoyed sprucing up the damaged backdrop and was seriously considering ordering some of the same shade to perk up the palace hallway which was beginning to look rather tatty. It was a big job which would require a substantial amount of scaffolding, but she was confident that she now had enough experience to manage well enough.

Back in the theatre, the canvas canopy had been covered with floating lengths of sparkling fabric gathered hastily from the wardrobe mistress, who had commissioned them for a previous production. Hung strategically, they gave the pleasing impression of an exotic desert tent. The whole effect was wonderfully dramatic from the moment the curtain was raised.

The Queen opened her programme with satisfaction, grateful that their combined skills had contributed to arriving successfully at this evening.

The King carefully removed a small spanner from his pocket which he'd brought, 'just in case', and which had been digging uncomfortably into his thigh.

His wife smiled to herself, and allowed the music to carry her away in her imagination to calmer days in which she would once more, lean on a gate and watch one of Slopingsideways's spectacular sunsets.

The Surprising Power of Cake

The Surprising Power of Cake

Nora Whittington-Fay heard the sharp crack of a pencil snapping.

The crunching sound resounded around her head because the pencil in question had been in her mouth at the time. Her habit of chewing the end of a writing implement while she was concentrating was one her mother had spoken to her about in no uncertain terms when she was still a child.

'Nora,' she had been told a bazillion times, 'you'll get splinters. Stop it at once; it's a filthy habit.'

Removing the shattered remnants from both her mouth and the dog-eared notepad in front of her, Nora frowned and sighed heavily. Her thoughts had been far away, and she was brought back to the present with a jolt.

She looked up from her workspace and was somewhat comforted by the familiar sight of the muddley garage, which she thought of as a creative palace, but always simply called, her workshop. In truth, it was a cross between a study, a laboratory and a studio, so workshop was an accurate name. The familiar sight of piles of books and papers, bits of dismantled machines, discarded diagrams, models and prototypes, flip charts, old coffee cups and general debris which was scattered around like rubbish the tide brings in twice a day, unsettled her not one bit. Here she spent many hours thinking, planning, experimenting, inventing and creating each day, before retreating back up the wonky stairs to her living space above. Had she been a grander person, she might have called that her apartment, but it was almost as muddley as the downstairs space and she had no such pointless pretensions.

Nora came from a long line of inventors who had achieved varying degrees of success over many generations. Her famous American ancestor, Samuel B. Fay, had invented the humble paperclip back in the 1860s. What an invention that had been – and still was! Such a simple little piece of bent wire became a worldwide phenomenon. The idea was ambitious and the solution so simple; yet no one else had ever thought of it. That was the key to it; that was the beauty of it.

Paperclips were the talk of the day. This was great news for Mr. Fay and indeed, for the whole family, since their fortunes immediately took a welcome lift as they headed inevitably towards the twentieth century. Samuel had, with his simple little invention, found the perfect solution to the problem of attaching tickets to fabric as well as to other papers. This was about the same time that the typewriter was invented, but before anyone had heard of barbed wire or that famous fizzy drink now found the world over. For the Fay family, it was a pivotal moment and a great boon for office workers everywhere.

Everyone loved this wonderful little tool. Paperclips were cheap to produce, but used in such vast quantities in offices, hospitals, court rooms, and homes around the world that they became a very welcome moneymaker. In time, people discovered that they could find other handy uses for their paperclips: you could use them to hang Christmas decorations on your festive tree; you could, at a push, use one as a hair slide. By straightening it out, enterprising DIY-ers found they could use one to unclog their sink, reopen the holes in a blocked salt cellar, get hairs out of a brush and even clean their nails afterwards. Not very hygienic, but fabulously useful. Forty years later, people began using them to fix broken zips, as well as for the purpose for which they were originally intended; and one hundred years after that, we're all still using them.

The Fay family enjoyed the boost to their income and their profile, but in time the inventor's name faded into history, as they so often do, even while that clever little piece of creative genius went from strength to strength. These days, as you know, you can buy paper clips very cheaply, in multiple sizes, and the old irritation of them going rusty has vanished, thanks to coloured plastic coverings.

But it was Samuel who had sown the seeds of possibility into his family for discovering new and better ways of doing ordinary things, if only you could think of them. Taking an ordinary problem and finding the solution by making something extraordinary.

As his offspring grew, left home, and scattered around the globe, some of them carried and nurtured the hope that one day they too would invent something else as brilliant as Samuel's paper clip.

Nora Whittington-Fay was one of them. Her father, just like his grandfather, great-grandfather and, indeed great-grandmother (when she wasn't baking mouth-watering cakes), who had moved to England in the early 1900s, had spent many hours puzzling over various projects none of which, unfortunately, gave the same scale of result.

Indeed, fortunes had been *almost* made, and *definitely* lost, in cycles of *almost* achievement and *definite* failure. As the years went past, the financial strain of all this increased considerably on the struggling descendants of Samuel B. Fay. Cars, luxuries and, occasionally, houses had all been surrendered to the bank from time to time, as loans that had helped keep them afloat needed repayment. Truth to tell, their financial advisers had not always given the family the full picture of their increasingly precarious predicament. While a series of bank managers had extended the repayment period several times, the inevitable day came, sometime in the 1970s, when the grand eight-bedroomed house at the end of Chestnut

Close became forfeit. By then, only Nora and her brother, Alexander, remained in the family home.

Tears were shed, furniture auctioned, paintings purchased by collectors, and knick-knacks snapped up by local buyers at a rather embarrassing garage sale. A final ginger and lemon cake was baked from the old family recipe and shared together, before Alexander left to join an internationally-funded expedition to find the legendary yeti in the Himalayas. Perhaps he would make his name in that field of endeavour. Apart from a hastily written postcard eight years ago, his sister had heard nothing more from him; she hoped he had found happiness amongst the peace-loving nomads of Tibet.

Nora, meanwhile, had just enough funds to purchase a rickety, old, two-storey farm building, which was where she now lived and pursued her various designs in the hope that one day she could produce something which would have the same sort of impact as those little metal paperclips had once done.

Having broken her latest pencil – they all ended up in shattered pieces thanks to that dreadful chewing habit – she pushed her scribblings aside and went back upstairs in search of a restorative cup of tea and a slice of cake. That, she hoped, might give her both the break and the energy she needed to carry on.

To be honest, she had rather hit a brick wall on her inventing journey, and wasn't sure how to continue. She had great aspirations for making a toilet roll replacer that could be used by every household in the country, continent, and wherever indoor plumbing was operational. Time and time again she had come across people – usually other women – who despaired that anyone in their family would ever learn to put a new loo roll into the bathroom mechanism (regardless of its simplicity), so that the next user would not be faced with the bleak prospect of an empty cardboard tube at the crucial moment.

Surely, she had told herself, this invention would be the one that propelled her back to prosperity and put her name amongst the great inventors chronicled in history books!

Nora had drawn detailed plans and created a working prototype but, having patented her design (a tiresome legal procedure that you will need to do if you want to make sure that no one steals your own brilliant idea and tries to pass it off as their own), she was coming to the unhappy realisation that the contraption was simply too large and unwieldy to be used in a domestic setting. Her invention was more like an industrialised dispenser; so, while it could helpfully store two dozen loo rolls at a time, no one would have room for their sink, or perhaps even their actual loo if it were installed in any other domestic toilet or bathroom. She was realistic enough to realise that this was counter-productive: a financial black hole, and total non-starter.

In fact, Nora wasn't doing any of this for the money. She was quite happy living above her messy workshop. She had no desire to purchase a big, fancy house that would require a lot of annoying maintenance and tiresome cleaning. Nora had no time for that sort of thing; her time was prioritised elsewhere. She would never waste her hard-earned profits in that way. She did, however, long to restore the good name of Samuel B. Fay amongst the community of inventors beavering away around the world.

Nora recognised that she wasn't, by nature, a tidy person – her thoughts were a continual whirlwind of puzzles and ideas and that was reflected in the muddlesome, yet comfortable, home she'd made for herself. Neither did Nora mind living alone. She enjoyed her own company. Besides, it gave her the great advantage of not having to observe

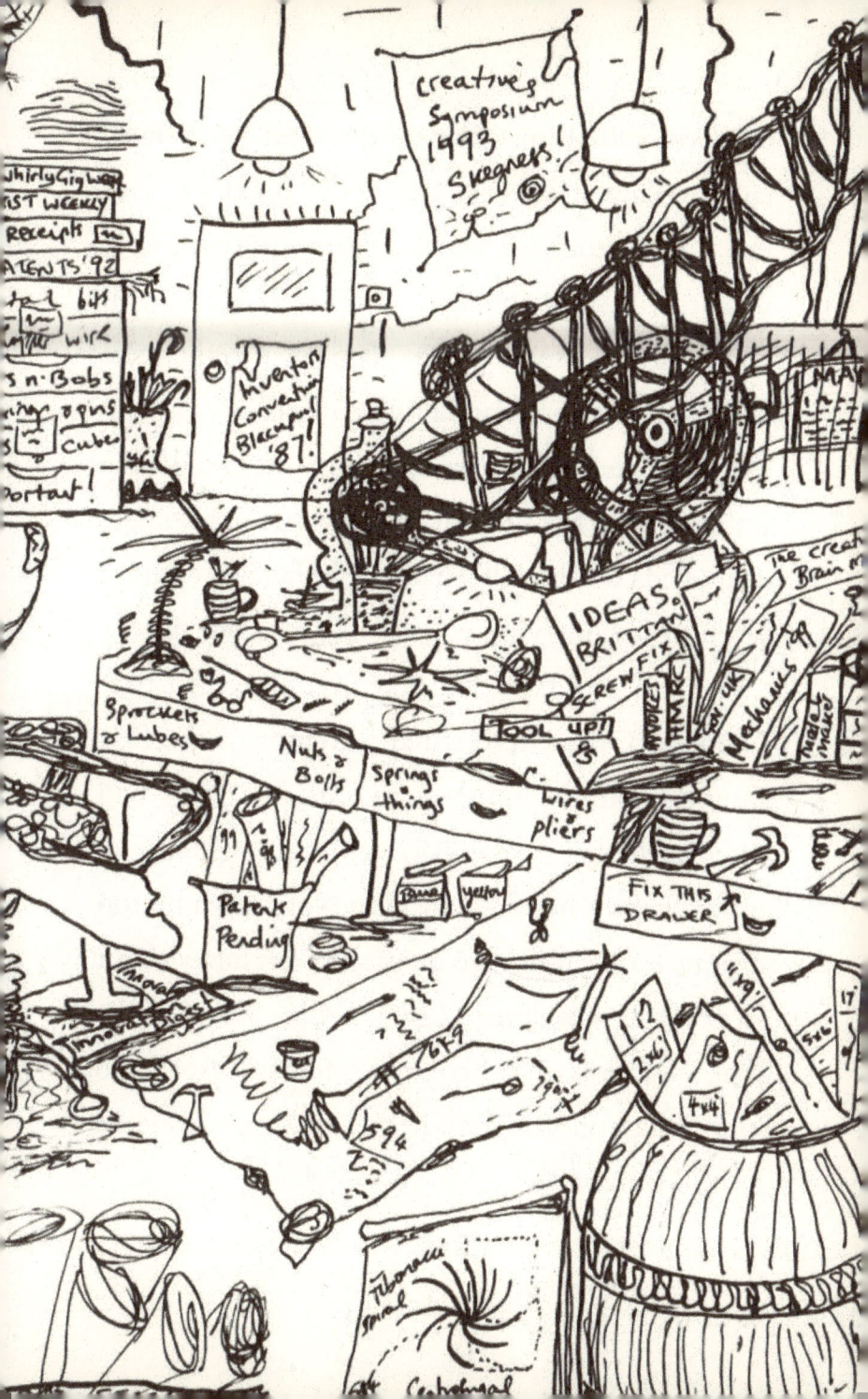

conventional things like meal times, bed times, laundry days or whether anyone else under her roof had a preference for which television programme to watch. If she wanted to get up at 3am and drill wood, or weld some pieces of metal together, she could do so without bothering anyone. Similarly, if she was wide awake after midnight, she could bake up a storm in the kitchen, clatter some pans, make cakes and cook herself whatever she fancied without creeping about trying not to wake someone else.

She had once had a cat called Otto (named after Nikolaus Otto, the German inventor of the first internal combustion engine), but the tabby had discovered that he could be fed more regularly at other people's houses. Life with Nora was a bit too chaotic for his liking, so one day he left her without so much as a backwards glance. Cats are a bit like that. Nora missed his company, but at least she no longer felt guilty about whether she'd remembered to feed him or not.

No, the real, horribly painful problem facing Nora was that all the good stuff had already been invented.

She spent wakeful nights pacing and chewing over this unpalatable fact in her mind, with and without a pencil in her mouth. Had you been a neighbour who shared her sleeplessness, you might have frequently observed her, staring out of one of the upstairs windows, scanning the night sky for inspiration and apparently mesmerised by the moon, neither of which offered her any help whatsoever.

If only she had been quicker off the mark, she repeatedly scolded herself, it could have been the name of Nora Whittington-Fay on escalators, chocolate fountains and colour televisions. Why, oh why, had she not thought of electric screwdrivers, food blenders or leaf blowers herself? Someone else had come up with microwaves, wet suits and umbrellas. It was not her name on laptop computers, paper shredders or sleeping bags. Radar was taken for granted these days, as were scissors, lawnmowers and plasters. Mobile phones, teabags and chocolate chips were old news. None of them, sadly, had sprung from the fertile imagination of Nora Whittington-Fay.

Stirring her tea thoughtfully, Nora reflected on all these things as she considered the last slice of coffee and walnut cake. It was rather too large to count as a single portion; on the other hand if she cut it in half she would have rather a stingy serving. It had been an exasperating morning, in the light of which she helped herself to the entire piece, decided it might possibly count as lunch, and closed the tin firmly. She couldn't quite face returning downstairs yet, so pushed aside a pile of *Innovation Digest* magazines, which were taking up most of the sofa space, and sat down gratefully.

Nora was nobody's fool, she knew that there must still be things that people needed; they just didn't know it yet. After all, that very famous IT chap had once insisted that people would need a middle sized computer; they just hadn't realised it, until he began producing them. Fellow computer buffs thought he was mad; but once they were available, people fell over themselves to buy the new gizmos which put yet more money into the over-stretched pockets of the inventor, who must have been laughing all the way to his bank. Nora's bank would like her to pull off a similar act of genius.

Obviously, *everybody* knew that cures for cancer, Alzheimer's, Ebola and other terrible diseases were still waiting to be found, but Nora, as I told you, was realistic and fully aware that she simply didn't have the level of medical knowledge required for such wonderful discoveries. Her skills lay elsewhere.

Putting her feet up on an upholstered stool, which was the last remnant of her parent's belongings, Nora munched on the delicious cake and closed her eyes to think. All those sleepless nights must have caught up with her, for before you could say, Alexander Graham Bell (the inventor of the telephone, after whom her brother had been named), she was fast asleep.

It was two and half hours later when she woke with a jerk – barely saving her half-eaten cake which had been balanced on her lap – by the insistent shriek of an alarm. Bleary and disoriented, she narrowly avoided kicking over her stone-cold tea as she stumbled towards the sound.

Nora's phone was going mad. She could hear it, but it took a while to locate it under a pile of bills and a large book advocating the possibilities and benefits of fish skin swimwear. Thankfully pressing the 'off' button, Nora peered at the screen.

'Bother!' she announced to the muddled mess around her, 'that means it's Wednesday. It's my day to fetch Toby from school. I totally forgot.'

Pulling on her boots and grabbing her coat, Nora headed quickly down the stairs and out into the damp afternoon. Toby was Nora's much-loved godson; a tousled-haired eight-year-old, who she spent time with every week. His grandmother was Nora's cousin which technically made him her third cousin, or possibly her first cousin twice removed – all rather complicated but, as you know, families can be very complicated. Toby's mother worked late on a Wednesday so the arrangement was that Nora would collect him from school and bring him back to her house from where he would be picked up around 6pm.

It was a good arrangement for Toby's mum, a nice diversion for Nora (so long as she set an alarm to remind her to walk down to the school), and a fascinating couple of hours for Toby, who loved the relaxed nature of Nora's life compared with his own. In his house, he was always having to tidy up, put his plate in the dishwasher, pick up his coat, leave his shoes neatly, and so on. Aunty Nora (that's what he called her; after all, 'third-cousin-Nora' is rather a mouthful), always had interesting things going on in her workshop, where weird and wonderful books showed strange diagrams and were scattered haphazardly, often open at pages with coloured pictures and graphs. Toby found it all very refreshing and looked forward to his weekly trip. He also looked forward to the cake.

Nora buttoned her coat as she walked which may be why, when she arrived a little late at the school gate, she looked somewhat dishevelled. Toby saw her coming, checked with his teacher and ran across the playground to meet her.

'Hello, Aunty Nora; you look funny!'

Toby was nothing if not honest. He eyed her carefully with his head on one side.

'It's because you've done your coat up wrong.'

He pointed to the buttons.

Nora looked down and realised that in her hurry she had missed a button and left the whole thing wonky. 'Not to worry; I'll sort it out as we walk.'

She was also wearing odd socks, but nobody could see those, and it wasn't the sort of thing she thought important anyway. Together they walked towards home.

Usually, Toby was full of stories from school, chatting animatedly about things they were learning, questions he had, ideas he was working on, and general chat. Today he seemed like one of those footballs that has been stored in the PE cupboard for too long, and collapses on itself. All his usual energy was gone – squished completely out of him – and, when Nora looked at him sideways, she saw that his eyes were red. Had he been crying? She was reluctant to ask him outright because she knew, as do you, that those sort of questions can clog the words in your throat and leave you feeling pretty uncomfortable. At the same time, Nora didn't want to ignore it. If her favourite, and only, godson was upset, she wanted to know; not because she was nosy, but because she wanted to help.

Wisely holding her tongue until they got home, Nora extracted the key from her pocket with a collection of tissues, cough sweets, rubber bands and paperclips. (Yes; she always had one to hand, just in case.) Together, they entered the workshop and clambered up the creaky stairs where they shrugged off their coats and collapsed in a grateful heap on the sofa amongst the crumpled magazines.

After a few moments of silence, during which it was clear that Toby wasn't going to speak, Nora got up again.

'Cake!' she announced decisively, and Toby immediately looked less like a crusty, half-pumped football.

Cake can be the solution to so many things and is always a great way to start a conversation; especially if it's going to be a tricky or painful one.

There was a moment of awkward stillness as Nora opened the tin and realised that, as you will have remembered, she had eaten the last slice for her not-lunch lunch. If she hadn't fallen asleep, she would have had time to make another, but right now she was staring at a sorry collection of crumbs in an otherwise empty tin.

'Hmmm,' she pondered; disappointed that she couldn't immediately resolve some of Toby's apparent unhappiness. However, she also knew, as do you, that not only do good things come to those who wait, but that food should never be a substitute for a sad feeling inside your insides.

Making a quick decision, she pulled a recipe book from her groaning shelves where it was rubbing shoulders with tomes on spark plugs in the 1950s, and manuals on making your own rocket.

'All hands on deck, Toby,' she announced, slipping into naval language. 'Owing to a logistical error, we're going to have to start from scratch. Choose a cake and let's make one together.'

Toby was more than happy with this arrangement. He was a great admirer of his godmother's cakes and looked forward to his weekly treat, but she had always chosen and baked in advance until today. There wasn't a choice of cake, although she knew he was as fond of chocolate as you are, and was careful to keep that in mind.

With a watery grin, he blew his nose, picked up the cookery book and searched the index in detail. There were Victoria sponge cakes and variations of chocolate themed goodies: brownies, flapjacks, shortbreads etc. He looked at pictures of carrot cakes, lemon cakes, Madeira cakes, red velvet cakes, coconut and pineapple cakes. They all looked wonderful, but the feeling in the pit of his stomach wasn't relieved by any of them; nothing seemed quite right today. A doctor, of course, always knows what the patient needs and prescribes medicine accordingly. We're not always quite so clear about what we need when we feel a bit 'off'.

Nora could see that nothing was jumping out at her godson.

'Tell you what,' she suggested, 'why don't you invent one of your own? After all, inventing is in your blood!'

Toby's eyes lit up.

'You know that the creative DNA inside me is inside you too, don't you?' she went on. 'I reckon you could come up with a stunningly fabulous cake.'

Toby nodded enthusiastically. Slipping off the stool where he'd been studying the book, he helped Nora gather weighing scales, a mixing bowl, and all the paraphernalia you need to bake a great cake. She turned the oven on in anticipation, and stood back to see what Toby would create.

Soon he was measuring quantities of butter and sugar, cracking eggs and sifting flour. This would be a magnificent cake, there was no doubt about that. He added pinches of this, splashes of that, sprinkles of something else, and drops of the other. There was such a lot of mixture after everything had been combined and stirred that there was actually enough for two cakes. They took the mixing in turns because, unless you have an electric mixer this part can be quite tough on your arms. I am not at all sure why, in the home of an inventor, there was not such a gadget; I can only assume that it was lying somewhere downstairs in several pieces, waiting to be repaired.

Toby was worried that his aunty might be cross that he had used so many of her ingredients and made such a massive amount of cake mixture; he knew his mother would have been.

'No problem,' Nora assured him. 'There's always a need for cake. Or, we could just have an extra large one to celebrate your first cake invention.'

So saying, she whipped out twice the usual number of prepared baking tins, filled them with Toby's wonderful mixture, popped them into the oven, and set a timer on her phone.

'Right then, let's go and see what's happening downstairs while it cooks.'

Toby was equally content with this suggestion. He loved browsing in the workshop and fiddling with the bits and pieces that were nestled in various tins and boxes. He would have been disappointed to miss that weekly pleasure if cooking cake took up all their time together before his mother arrived.

Side-by-side, Nora showed Toby what she was working on. The toilet roll replacer was examined in detail but he could only agree that it was never going to work in a normal bathroom.

Ideas-people usually work on more than one project at a time, and Nora was no exception.

'What do you think of this?' she asked, pulling a diagram out from under another pile of books and oily rags.

Toby looked at the picture, then turned it sideways and looked again.

'What is it?' he asked.

Nora tutted, and turned it back the right way up.

'It's an idea for a shopping trolley that returns itself.'

Toby studied the plan, noting the mechanism and reading all the labels scrawled in Nora's familiar hand writing.

'That's a good idea,' agreed Toby. 'People hate taking their trolleys back. I suppose that's why supermarkets started making you put a coin in to use them.'

'True,' Nora confirmed, 'but it's not ideal is it? What if you don't have the right coin? People use plastic bank cards to pay these days, and you can't fit a week of shopping into a basket.'

She was right about that. Toby hated carrying the basket for his mum; it always bashed his legs, and if she bought tins or bottles it got super-heavy really fast. A trolley was much better.

'I've based it on an electric golf bag. Have you seen those?' Nora asked.

Toby shook his head.

'I noticed them a few months ago when I passed the golf course on the other side of town. The golfers weren't pushing or pulling them; the bags are designed so they propel themselves up or down hills on the course. I think perhaps golfers aren't strong enough to haul them round eighteen holes.'

Toby laughed, imagining puny golfers struggling with bags of golf clubs which were almost as big as they were, arriving on the smooth greens thoroughly out of breath from their exertions, and barely able to swing their clubs.

Before long their two heads were bent closely together examining Nora's next plan, and Toby began to seem more like himself again.

Clever Nora knew that it's easier to talk about difficult things when you sit next to someone, not opposite them. Pushing her chair back a little she looked at her godson who was still engrossed in the invention plans.

'If only every problem was so easy to solve,' she said. 'There's a whole bunch of stuff I'd like to invent but it's just beyond me.'

'What do you mean,' asked Toby, looking up briefly from beneath his fringe which was flopping forward as he leant into the work table. 'What would you like to invent?'

'Well, let me think… A solution to bad manners for a start. I'd be delighted to create an invention to stop people sniffing, or eating with their mouths open, or talking in the cinema. Imagine if we could come up with something to make people always put their rubbish in a bin, to solve traffic problems, or to help people find the end of a roll of sticky tape. These are everyday problems.' She paused reflectively. 'What would you like to invent?'

The question hung in the air for a while.

'I think I'd like to invent something that blocks speed cameras,' Toby said decidedly. His mother had received a speeding fine just that week, and was extremely cross about it. Consequently, she had been distracted and burnt the sausages she was cooking for his tea. Toby had had to scrape off the blackest bits and crunch his way through the rest.

Nora laughed.

'That would be very popular,' she agreed. 'What else?'

Toby shuffled restlessly; clearly he had something on his mind.

'I wish we could invent a pill that would make people kind.'

'Ah,' Nora realised that they were getting to the heart of the problem at last. She paused.

'Trouble at school?'

Toby swiped at his eyes, irritated to find that they had started watering quite of their own accord. He nodded, reluctant to say more in case he embarrassed himself by crying again. His former tears had been shed in the privacy of the cloakroom where he'd managed to get them under control before lining up at the end of the day; now, he wasn't so sure he could keep them at bay.

The timer rang on Nora's phone, which broke the tension he was feeling.

'Let's go and find that cake,' his aunt said, not pushing him for more information.

Upstairs, they found a cooling tray and Nora carefully carried the works of culinary art to the counter. Tapping the tins firmly, she turned each of them upside down to reveal a perfect set of coffee, chocolate sponges.

'Those look amazing!'

Toby glowed with pleasure.

'Let's hope they taste as good as they look!'

He was in charge of icing and decorating and, while he worked, he began to tell Nora about what had been going on at school. She let him talk while she made a fresh pot of tea.

It turned out that two of the bigger sporty boys, Max and Milo, had been picking on him. Toby had done all the usual things you're supposed to do: ignored them, stood up to them, told a teacher; nothing made a difference. Today they had got hold of his special book where he worked on his own inventions: ideas for wonderful toys and machines that could do jobs for you that you didn't want to do, like picking up laundry and folding clothes. He was secretly hoping that he could make a robot that would do his homework for him, or even go to school for him so he could work on his ideas all the time, like Aunty Nora did.

He finished his story at the same time as balancing the biggest strawberry on top of the cake. It truly was an amazing cake. Four sponges stacked on top of each other, decorated with

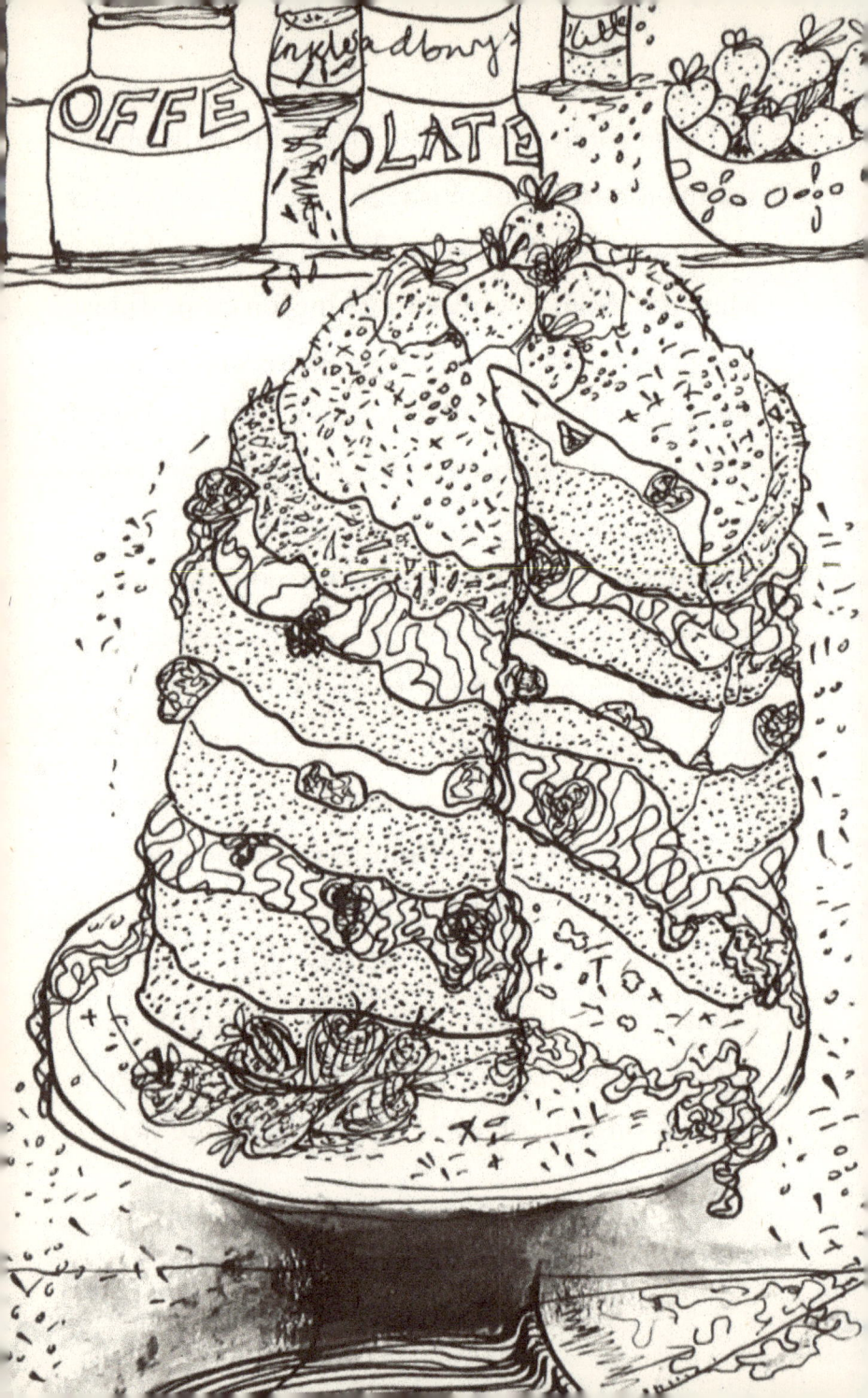

sprinkles, circled with strawberries and edible glitter, and stuck together with alternating layers of jam and whipped cream.

'I think we should take a picture of this one,' said Nora, reaching for her phone again. 'I've never made anything as fabulous as this. It's totally unique, Toby!'

With the picture taken, she lifted one of her sharpest knives from the drawer and handed it to Toby.

'Let's see how it tastes.'

Cautiously, Toby sliced into the beautiful cake revealing coloured layers of sponge inside. It really was a work of art. It was also tricky to transfer a slice on to a plate without the whole thing disintegrating but, with a few wobbles, he managed it.

'So,' said Nora tucking into her first mouthful ' – oh my; this is incredible Toby. Stunning and fabulous, as I predicted!'

He smiled, his own mouth crammed full of the fantastic cake. He daren't speak in case it all came tumbling out, but she was right. It was *very* good.

'So,' Nora resumed, 'you want to invent a pill to make people kind.' She looked fondly at her godson.

'It's a genius idea, Tobes; it really is.'

Nora took another very unladylike mouthful of cake before saying anything else. Perhaps Toby should turn his hand to inventing dishes in the kitchen rather than in a workshop. He definitely had talent.

'The thing is,' she said, after swallowing and taking a sip of hot tea, 'I don't think it will work.'

Toby frowned. His aunt was usually so encouraging; why would she smoosh his idea before it began? He absolutely knew it was a brilliant idea. He already planned to slip one into Max and Milo's lunch.

'Why not?' he asked moodily. 'It would make far more difference than any box of paper clips ever will.'

'You're right; I know you are, Toby. That's not the difficulty.'

'What then?'

Toby accidentally spat a few crumbs out as he responded to her.

'Sorry,' he muttered, picking them off the counter and popping them back into his mouth.

There was another pause, and he could see Nora was thinking hard, not just dismissing his idea.

'Well, kindness comes from the inside, not the outside, doesn't it?' she asked.

Toby said nothing. He wondered where she was going with this.

'What I mean is, all the inventions in the world that have ever helped people, have been things that *do* something; which is great. But, you have to *be* kind. No one can do it for you; we can't stick it on someone or plant it inside them like a special tube that helps hearts beat better, or blood vessels to stay open. Unkind people need to change their minds, or maybe it's their hearts; either way, something on the inside has to *be* different. To *be* better; to *be* kind.'

Another silence fell on the kitchen.

What Aunty Nora said made sense. Toby knew she was right, he just didn't *want* her to be right. It was hard to hear that his idea couldn't work. He really wanted to sort out those boys who were making his life at school so miserable.

'I wish we could invent it Toby, I really do; with all my heart.'

Toby felt his aunt's hand comfortingly on his back. He wished it too, with his whole being, like nothing he'd ever wished before.

'I don't know what to do,' he admitted. 'I've tried everything. Any ideas?' he added, hopefully.

Nora drew a deep breath and squeezed his shoulder.

'Well, it's not foolproof by any means; but I do have one idea we could try.'

Toby pushed his fringe out of his eyes, wiped his nose briefly on his sleeve (something his mother would have reprimanded him for, and usually his godmother too), and looked for some kind of solution in Nora's expression.

She nodded thoughtfully and turned his plate around to view the remains of his first slice from a different angle.

'Cake.'

'What? I mean, pardon?' He corrected himself. His godmother was very keen on good manners.

Nora nodded her head at him and pointed to the products of their combined labour.

'Seriously; cake.'

She sounded quite pleased with herself.

'You'd be surprised at the restorative power of a simple, or even a very complicated, cake!'

Toby felt a smile playing around his mouth. He wasn't going to argue about cake, but what exactly did she have in mind?

The next half hour was spent discussing a plan. To begin with Toby resisted.

'There's no way that will work,' he declared, with certainty.

Nora shrugged. 'We'll never know if we don't try.'

Eventually they came to an agreement and Nora fetched a writing pad and envelopes. Toby wrote out two almost identical notes and sealed the envelopes with a crummy lick, just as his mum rang the doorbell to take him home, and he quickly slipped them into his school bag.

The week passed slowly and the next Wednesday, with the smell of freshly baked cake hanging in the air, Nora set several alarms to make sure she didn't forget her appointment at school.

Half an hour afterwards, neighbours would have noticed her returning home with not one, but three young lads. What they wouldn't have been able to see was the way they all eagerly tucked into a selection of home-baked cakes together. Neither would they have observed the way the two extra guests engaged, wide-eyed and fascinated as Nora and Toby introduced them to the workshop. They looked at books, asked questions about diagrams, fiddled with prototypes and left not only full of cake, but keen to return.

I wish I could tell you that Max and Milo, for that is who the guests were as I'm sure you have guessed, were never unkind again. That would not be entirely true, but they were never unkind to Toby. Not only did they stop bullying him, but their parents allowed them to visit Nora some Wednesday afternoons after school, where she encouraged them to think of solutions to a number of problems, including the age-old challenge of being kind to others. After all, if that were solved a great many other problems in the world would also be fixed.

She pushed some of the worst of the muddley muddle into large boxes to set aside some space for them in the workshop so they could do some inventing of their own. It soon became a place of great activity, creativity and friendship. In fact, it wasn't long before Nora was asked to set up an after-school club for young inventors, which was extremely popular.

They never did manage to come up with anything that could give old Samuel B. Fay's paperclips a run for their money, but they did have a lot of fun.

And always, without fail, there was cake.

The End